...ng?"

"Staying, of course," she answered in a clipped tone. "I can scarcely swim back to L.A."

"No? I thought maybe you could, being a mermaid and all."

"I've had about enough of the mermaid subject," Lisa said in exasperation. "I'd like to forget last night, the stupid commercial and the ridiculous costume."

"You can forget it if you like," he teased, "but I have no intention of doing so. How many men can claim to have met a mermaid in the flesh? I think . . . I'd like to find out how it feels to kiss one."

SONDRA STANFORD
wrote advertising copy before trying her hand at romantic fiction. Also an artist, she enjoys attending arts and crafts shows and browsing at flea markets. Sondra and her husband live happily with their two children in Corpus Christi, Texas.

Dear Reader:

Romance readers have been enthusiastic about Silhouette Special Editions for years. And that's not by accident: Special Editions were the first of their kind and continue to feature realistic stories with heightened romantic tension.

The longer stories, sophisticated style, greater sensual detail and variety that made Special Editions popular are the same elements that will make you want to read book after book.

We hope that you enjoy this Special Edition today, and will enjoy many more.

The Editors at Silhouette Books

SONDRA STANFORD
For All Time

Silhouette Special Edition
Published by Silhouette Books New York
America's Publisher of Contemporary Romance

SILHOUETTE BOOKS, a Division of Simon & Schuster, Inc.
1230 Avenue of the Americas, New York, N.Y. 10020

Distributed by Pocket Books

ISBN: 0-671-53687-7

First Silhouette Books printing September, 1984

10 9 8 7 6 5 4 3 2 1

Map by Ray Lundgren

SILHOUETTE, SILHOUETTE SPECIAL EDITION and
colophon are registered trademarks of Simon & Schuster, Inc.

America's Publisher of Contemporary Romance

Printed in the U.S.A.

BC91

Books by Sondra Stanford

Silhouette Romance

Golden Tide #6
Shadow of Love #25
Storm's End #35
No Trespassing #46
Long Winter's Night #58
And Then Came Dawn #88
Yesterday's Shadow #100
Whisper Wind #112
Tarnished Vows #131

Silhouette Special Edition

Silver Mist #7
Magnolia Moon #37
Sun Lover #55
Love's Gentle Chains #91
The Heart Knows Best #161
For All Time #187

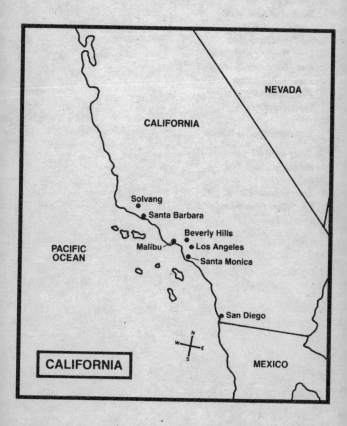

Chapter One

$\mathcal{D}$usk was falling, deepening the shadows along the canyon road. The spring California evening was chilly and Lisa Knight wished she'd had the foresight to grab a sweater before she'd left the apartment. The absurd costume she wore was skimpy and did nothing to protect her from the elements. Goose bumps covered her arms and she sighed, wishing she didn't need the extra bit of money this evening would bring. Of course, if she had refused, she knew she'd never be hired by the Mouton Advertising Agency again, and while it would be nice not to need such extra work from time to time, reality dictated otherwise. The independence she sought in her free-lance writing career had thus far not materialized.

At that instant she heard a loud thud beneath the car and a moment later felt a telltale pull toward the right.

A flat.

Lisa immediately pulled to the edge of the road, as far off as she dared, and cut the motor. She felt near tears over her situation and bent her head forward to rest it against the steering wheel. Her strawberry-blond hair billowed about her face and swished against her bare shoulders. Now what was she going to do? It was bad enough that she scarcely remembered the tire-changing lesson her father had given her years ago; now she would not only be late for the party, but when she did arrive, she would be filthy and grease-stained. Dusty Mouton, the owner of the agency, would be livid at having his surprise ruined.

She raised her head and peered into the gathering gloom. No houses or lights were to be seen, but even if they were there, they were probably so well concealed behind trees that she couldn't see them. And from what she could judge, Dusty's house was probably still a good three-quarters of a mile farther down the road.

Brooding wasn't accomplishing anything; resolutely, Lisa took the flashlight from the glove compartment, grabbed her keys and got out of the car.

She opened the trunk and, straining her five-foot-three frame while tottering on dangerously high heels, one foot on pavement, the other sunken in the grass, pulled out the jack. She had just bent to lower it to the ground when a car rounded the bend from behind her, its two bright headlights pinning her against the car as though she were a mounted specimen in a museum.

The car had been moving fast and its lights swept past her, on to illuminate dark trees, but the driver suddenly braked and red taillights gleamed as the car backed up, coming to a halt at the side of the road just in front of Lisa's car.

A man approached, and as he drew near they could see each other clearly in the waning gray light from the sky. He was a very tall man by any standard, but to Lisa he seemed overwhelmingly enormous. He had a shock of thick dark hair and he was dressed in formal dinner clothes. Lisa had an impression of power, immense vitality and incredible good looks all wrapped up in one giant-sized body.

He stopped near the left fender of her car and stared hard at Lisa. The eyes, dark as the canyon shadows, seemed to scorch her skin as he surveyed her with insulting and frightening deliberation. Not that she could altogether blame him. She knew well enough what a fool she looked as those piercing eyes took in every detail from her skintight gold-mesh skirt, which tapered to her ankles and was covered with gold metallic "scales," the blue-gray "seaweed" bikini bra, the shell necklace and earrings, right up to the pink-tinted, fluted plastic shell she wore in her hair.

Suddenly he tossed back his head and roared with laughter. "Aren't you a little off the beaten path for a mermaid?" he teased in a deep, amused voice. "What're you trying to do, cause mortal men to kill themselves on this dangerous curve by looking at yours instead?"

Lisa went hot and cold all at once. If she could have sunk into a hole and disappeared right then, she would have done just that. Nervously, she raised her arms and crossed them in front of her breasts, the only defense she had.

"Go away," she said in a low voice, altogether ignoring the fact that here was a big, strong man who might possibly change her tire for her. She hated him, hated that derisive smirk on his lips and the laughter that was still rumbling through him.

"Are you sure that's what you want?" he taunted. "Or don't mermaids need help changing their flat tires?"

Before she could respond, another car swept around the curve. As soon as the headlights picked Lisa out of the shadows, there were whistles and catcalls. The car slowed, but when the lights revealed the huge man standing near her, it speeded up again and took off.

Lisa shivered, but it was from nerves, not the chill of the evening. Standing half-naked like this on the side of the road, she was prey to every kind of insult, not to mention danger. Why, why didn't the earth mercifully open up and swallow her?

The man noticed her tremble. Since the second car had passed, he was no longer laughing. With a frown, he whipped off his jacket, strode forward and wrapped it around her, saying in a strangely angry voice, "Here, cover yourself up, for God's sake! And from now on it might be better for you to drive around with a bit more clothes on, unless, that is, you happen to *like* being leered at and possibly even getting attacked."

"You're crude and disgusting!" she snapped hotly.

He smiled. "Possibly. I am only a man, after all. But it seems to me you're inviting a whole lot of trouble if you're going to go out in public wearing such a seductive outfit. Now why don't you be a good little girl and go sit in the car while I change your tire?'' Without another word, he turned and went to the trunk to pull out the spare.

Totally demoralized, Lisa did as he told her. Standing on the side of the road as darkness fell and wearing such a risqué costume held no attraction for her, contrary to what her hateful rescuer had intimated.

She sat hunched in the front seat of her car while the man changed the tire. Nothing was going right for her these days, she thought dejectedly. Though she had sold three articles recently, she hadn't been paid for any of them yet and her bank balance was shrinking perilously low. That was why she'd auditioned for the Mermaid Shampoo TV commercial when a friend who worked at the Mouton Advertising Agency in Los Angeles had told her about it. Sometimes she thought she must be a masochist for having tried so hard to establish herself as a free-lance magazine writer. It was an impossibly precarious way to earn a living and that was why she now so desperately hoped she would land the job as West Coast correspondent for *Today's Journal*. If she got it, she'd still be able to write, but she'd also be drawing a regular paycheck like normal people—and she was certainly going to need that sort of security once her roommate, Veronica Wallace, got married. Things like rent and utility bills had to be paid on time and once Roni was gone, she wasn't going to have a financial backup anymore to tide her over the rough stretches whenever an expected check was late.

Roni, bless her, was also responsible for Lisa's chance

at the *Today's Journal* job. She worked in the office of the Cameron Children's Foundation and only a week ago had given Lisa a confidential tip about a large, secret donation that would make a great article. Lisa had immediately queried the magazine editor, to whom she'd previously sold several articles. The editor thought it was a terrific subject and had told her that if she was able to come up with the story, he'd like to discuss hiring her on as a regional stringer.

There was only one hitch and Lisa frowned, thinking about it. For the past week she'd been trying to reach Anthony Neugent at his office, with absolutely no luck. She supposed she had made a mistake when she'd identified herself as a reporter, or maybe he was simply allergic to telephone calls from unknown women. Whatever the reason, she had never been able to get past his secretary.

Today she had gone to his office in person and had overheard the secretary tell someone on the phone that he would be away at his ranch until Monday. Lisa wondered if she dared try to seek the illusive philanthropist there. She'd been toying with the idea all afternoon. Roni had told her where the ranch was located one day after her boss had visited it. But if Anthony Neugent didn't want to see her at his office, he wasn't likely to be any more receptive to her if she approached him while he was relaxing at home, and Lisa wondered whether it was a very smart idea. Still, she thought, she had nothing to lose by trying and she would most definitely lose the job opportunity with *Today's Journal* if she didn't get the interview.

With a thud, the trunk lid went down. Lisa got out of the car once more and slid the exquisitely tailored dinner jacket from her shoulders as the man, sleeves rolled to the elbows, came toward her, wiping his hands on what a little while ago had been a snowy-white handkerchief. The interior light of the car fell upon him, revealing a couple of dark smudges on his shirt as well. Lisa was appalled.

"You've ruined your shirt," she said with a sinking heart. It was bad enough to realize that now she owed the stranger the price of a new and probably very expensive shirt; he would also have to go wherever he was headed for the evening less than impeccably attired. There was no getting around the fact that it was her fault. "If you'll tell me how much it cost, I'll write you a check to cover it." She reached back inside the car for her handbag.

"Forget it," the man said in a gruff voice. "I'm sure the cleaners will be able to take out the stains." He began to roll down his shirt-sleeves.

"Please," Lisa said unhappily. "I'd feel much better if you would allow me to pay you for it. After all, you did me a favor by changing my tire."

The man stepped forward so that they were quite close and took his jacket from her hand. His face held a curious expression as he gazed down at her. "A sexy mermaid with scruples," he murmured half under his breath. "What an unusual combination." He shrugged the jacket over his massive shoulders while his eyes once more openly surveyed her semiclad body.

The suggestiveness of his gaze wiped away both Lisa's gratitude for what he had done for her and the guilt she felt over his soiled shirt. Sizzling resentment burned through her. "I've offered to make good my obligation," she said curtly. "Either take it or drop dead!" Whirling around, she got into the car and closed the door so that the interior light went off, concealing her body from further scrutiny.

The man chuckled. "That's what I like, a nice 'thank you' from a lady when I've done her a favor." He stepped away from the car window, gave her a mock salute and without another word strode toward the silver Porsche parked a few yards away.

Lisa watched as the other car's taillights came on, and a moment later it vanished around a bend in the road. She shivered and drew a long, deep breath, trying to get her own emotions under control. The man had been so obnoxious, had needled her so much, that she'd lost all civility. As he had pointed out at the end, she hadn't even bothered to thank him and the truth was she'd owed him gratitude for more than just changing the tire. If that other car with a group of men had stopped instead . . . Lisa shuddered even to think of it. Yet she had lost the opportunity to thank him and now she would never see him again.

Sighing, she started her car and drove on toward her destination. She was calmer by the time she reached the Mouton house. Already a lot of cars were there, which meant the party must be well under way. When she parked, Lisa glanced at her watch. She was twenty minutes late. She hoped Dusty hadn't given up on her and gone ahead without her.

Dusty Mouton opened the door himself. "Thank heaven!'' he breathed when he saw her standing there. ''We're almost ready for you girls to do your act and I was getting frantic!'' Grabbing her arm, he pulled her inside and closed the door. ''Where the hell have you been?''

''I had a flat,'' Lisa explained.

''Wonderful timing,'' Dusty said unsympathetically. ''You've set my ulcer back a year!'' Tugging on her arm, he led her through a side door, away from the room in which Lisa could see many of the party's guests mingling, and out to a patio.

There they joined the other two girls who had participated in the Mermaid Shampoo commercial. Cammie and Eve, a blonde and a brunette respectively, greeted Lisa warmly, and with impatience Dusty said, ''Okay, let's get ready. Go over to the other side of the pool. You'll take your positions with the light off and when Mr. Gate comes out we'll turn on the spotlight we've rigged up and you'll go into your song.''

The three girls straggled around the kidney-shaped swimming pool. ''If you ask me,'' Eve murmured, ''this is a stupid birthday surprise, even if it is for the chairman of the board of the corporation that produces Mermaid Shampoo. After all, he's seen the tapes of the commercial.''

''Don't knock it,'' Cammie said as she smoothed her long golden locks with her hand. ''We're getting paid extra for it, stupid or not, and that's all that concerns me. Besides, this looks like a crowd with money. It ought to be fun mingling. Who knows, maybe some of the men are unattached.''

Lisa shrugged, uninterested. "I just want to get this over with and go home. I've had a lousy day."

Five minutes later the floodlights around the pool were extinguished. The only lights remaining were gaily colored lanterns strung around the patio across the pool. From their vantage point in the darkness, the girls could see the guests emerge from the house.

"We've got a little birthday treat for you, Mr. Gate," Dusty's wife said to the man she led to the center of the patio.

"What is this?" the short, portly man said good-naturedly. "You planning to toss me into the pool?"

All the guests laughed, and from a concealed position behind a nearby bush the girls heard Dusty say in a stage whisper, "This is it! Positions, girls!"

The band hired for the evening swung into the familiar backup musical score from the commercial. The three girls struck their poses before the microphone and, when the spotlight came on, launched into their jingle which enumerated the virtues of Mermaid Shampoo while they swayed seductively and ran shapely hands through their long tresses.

The little performance was a hit with Mr. Gate. He roared with laughter and applauded vigorously as the other guests joined in. Then he rose from his chair, clasped Dusty Mouton on the shoulder and said, "Great idea, Dusty! The girls are even more beautiful in the flesh than they are on film!" He ambled around the pool and gave each girl an enthusiastic kiss on the cheek.

A photographer appeared to snap a few photos of him

standing with his arms around them, and when that was over Mr. Gate said, "Come with me, ladies. The band's about to start the dance music. I'm sure there must be a lot of eager males just dying to ask you to dance with them."

As a number of couples got up to dance, Mr. Gate escorted them to a small knot of men and, grinning, waved his hand expansively. "Here they are, gentlemen," he said grandly. "The lovely highlights of the evening. I promised them dance partners."

Lisa hung back a little, hating the whole thing and wishing she could decently escape. She glanced beyond Mr. Gate's left shoulder toward the group of men and an electrifying shock zipped through her. Looking at her with that awful, knowing grin on his face was the same man who had stopped to change her tire!

Somehow, the others melted away. The man stepped forward and slightly inclined his head. "May I have this dance?" he asked with meticulous, perfect manners.

Lisa knew that beneath the veneer of excessive politeness he was mocking her. She cringed inwardly and knotted her fists at her side, wondering how to get out of this.

He seemed to read her thoughts because he gave a thin smile. "Why don't you just say it and get it over with?" he suggested.

"Say what?" Lisa's green eyes narrowed warily.

"Drop dead. Go to hell. Whatever it is you're itching to tell me."

For answer, she glared at him, reminding herself she was at a party—a party, moreover, where she was one of the attractions rather than an invited guest—and that it wouldn't go over very well if she told off a legitimate guest.

When he saw that she wasn't going to say anything, the man held out his arms. Lisa was perfectly aware that he was putting her on the spot and it frustrated her beyond measure. She would make herself as well as him look ridiculous if she refused to dance now. With extreme reluctance, she placed her left hand on his shoulder and her right hand in his left. Slowly, they began to move in time to the soft, romantic tune that until this minute had been one of Lisa's favorites.

"I don't know very much about mermaids," he said after a moment. "Tell me, are they this tense and prickly, not to mention rude and unfriendly, just when they're out of the water, or are they always this way?"

Lisa had to tip back her head a long way to look up at him. From this position, she could see the fiery gleam of teasing in his deep-brown eyes and the laugh lines that fanned outward from them. She could see a tiny scar on his right temple just above his thick eyebrow and she couldn't help but notice the appealingly deep indentations in his cheeks whenever he smiled. The man was too good-looking for his own good, she thought sourly, and was very well aware of it. Women probably fell at his feet in droves and the reason he kept on taunting her was because she had been a lone holdout. But it would be a blistering February morning at the North Pole before she caved in and gave him the satisfaction he wanted.

"Look," she began coldly, "I appreciate what you did for me back there on the road and I'm still willing to pay for your shirt if you like. Pay for what you did, as well. But that doesn't mean I have to like you, so can we please just shut up and finish this dance?''

''Whatever you like,'' he said agreeably. Without warning, he drew her close so that her head was nestled against his wide, rock-hard chest, just beneath his chin. He dropped her hand and wrapped both his arms tightly around her, fitting their bodies into intimate nearness.

A flood of strange feelings spread through Lisa . . . of warmth, of languor, of sensual pleasure. It was as though she belonged where she was, cuddled in this large man's arms, feeling the heat of his body pressed to hers, savoring the clean scent of him, taking a strange delight in rubbing her cheek against the smooth fabric of his jacket.

One of his hands went up to touch her hair and then his fingers threaded through it. ''So soft and beautiful,'' he whispered as he bent his head to touch the crown of hers. ''No wonder you were chosen for the commercial. You'll sell millions of bottles of shampoo and you'll have at least half the men in the country wishing they could run their hands through your hair the way I'm doing and then make love to you . . . just the way I'd like to do.''

His comment brought Lisa down to earth again. He was holding her entirely too close and she was enjoying the sensation of it far too much! It was ridiculous. She didn't even know this man and here she was allowing him to hold her as though they were indeed lovers! She pulled herself away, forcing him to give her space. ''I . . . Don't say things like that to me,'' she ordered unsteadily.

''Why not?'' he asked. His mouth quirked upward in a derisive smile. ''The way you're dressed, the way you look, I'm sure every man here tonight feels the same way. Surely you ought to be flattered. It's what you want, isn't it? To entice men? If you didn't, you wouldn't have accepted the job.''

"That's not true!" Lisa hissed under her breath. "In the first place, my costume isn't *that* daring! It'll be seen on family television, for goodness' sake! And in the second place, I took the job for the same reason anyone else would have, to earn a living! I'm not out to 'entice' men, and I resent your inference very much! Besides, who named you judge and jury over my motives about absolutely anything?" She glared at him, seething with resentment. The man had been a thorn in her side all evening and she'd just about had all his needling she could take!

"I'll bet I know what the trouble is!" he said suddenly with an air of someone having just received a divine oracle from the gods. "There's probably no mermen in the sea, so that makes mermaids get all crotchety and mean. Is that why you had to come to land? To seek a man?" He shook his head. "Of course, if that's your intention, you're going to have to work on that disposition of yours. Just because you're sexy as all get-out, that doesn't . . ."

Abruptly, he was talking to thin air, but he didn't seem to mind. Lisa heard him chuckling softly as she stalked away.

She headed straight for the house, but just as she reached the doorway Dusty popped up, seemingly out of nowhere. "Where're you going?"

"Home."

He shook his head. "Not yet. Mr. Gate wants a dance with each of his 'mermaids.'" He chuckled. "My idea for a birthday surprise went over big. Gate thinks when the commercial airs, it'll be very successful. If it is, it'll be a feather in all our caps," he ended proudly.

"I hope it is," Lisa said politely, in fact not caring in the least. "Look, Dusty, I'd really like to leave now. I have a headache. Besides, sticking around to dance wasn't part of the deal."

"Half an hour," Dusty pleaded. "Come on, Lisa, be a sport. The other girls don't seem to mind." They both glanced toward the dancers and saw Eve and Cammie with their partners. Since they were smiling, it did look as though they were enjoying themselves.

"I'm not in a party mood," Lisa stated doggedly.

"Just hang around until you've had a chance to dance with Mr. Gate," Dusty said. "That's all I ask."

Lisa looked at him. As far as she was concerned, the Mermaid Shampoo thing was no longer important, as long as she got paid for her part. She had no interest in buttering up Mr. Gate, even if he was a wealthy and important man. But she sensed the underlying desperation in Dusty's voice. The happier he made a big client like Mr. Gate, the better off his career would be. He was really asking very little of her and besides, she liked Dusty. There was no sense making things hard on him just because she was being tormented by the big giant who had taken it upon himself to bedevil her tonight.

After a moment, she nodded and smiled. "Okay, Dusty, I'll stay. But only for a while."

"Good girl!" He grinned and patted her shoulder. "I knew you wouldn't let me down."

For the next half hour or so, Lisa was kept busy dancing

and making the inevitable inane conversation people indulge in at parties. She smiled so much her face was beginning to ache, but she kept it up for Dusty's sake.

Although she didn't dance again with the man who'd changed her flat, she could not help but notice him dancing with other women and seeming to be having a grand time. Probably thought he was God's gift to women, she thought scornfully. Not only did he seem to be enjoying himself, but she couldn't help but see that his partners were all smiles as well, including Cammie. Obviously his disapproval of Lisa's attire didn't extend to Cammie, who was dressed identically, because she was laughing and giving him overtly invitational messages with her eyes. Lisa looked away, disgusted.

Still, for all he appeared to like the way Cammie was dressed, the man continued to look down on her. Twice, while she was dancing with other men, her eyes happened to connect with his. Each time he was frowning and looking at her like a wrathful father. As though anything she did were his business! The idea enraged Lisa and both times she immediately turned her attention back to her dance partner and favored him with the brightest smile she could muster.

It was all a strain on her nerves, though. No matter what she was doing or with whom she was speaking, even once when she stood talking to middle-aged Mrs. Gate, she felt the man's eyes on her. She had never wanted to hit someone so badly in her life and it took every ounce of restraint not to turn around and scream at him like a shrew.

Mr. Gate, the guest of honor, had a fine time dancing

with every woman at the party, but finally it was Lisa's turn. With infinite gratitude, she accompanied him to the dance floor and did her best to block out of her mind the pair of dark eyes she knew were on her. Her skin prickled beneath the impact of that gaze.

But at last the dance ended. As soon as Mr. Gate turned his attention elsewhere, Lisa made good her escape.

In front of the house she walked quickly toward her car. She had just reached it and placed her hand on the door handle when a dark form emerged from the black shadows of hedges around the side of the house. Lisa gasped and then the form took shape as a man stepped forward into the semilight cast from the house. Naturally it was none other than her tormentor.

"Leaving so soon?" he asked idly. "The party won't be the same without you."

"I know." Lisa trembled with hostility. "You'll have to find someone else whose evening you can spoil."

He ignored that. "We never did introduce ourselves," he told her.

"There would be no point to it," Lisa snapped. "I hope I never set eyes on you again as long as I live."

The man smiled, unperturbed. "Well, I know I'll be seeing you again . . . on television. I'm sure the commercial will lead you far toward an acting career. You're the sexiest one of the three, as I'm sure you're well aware of and gratified to know, considering all the attention you received tonight from the men back there." He pointed a thumb over his shoulder toward the house. "I'll bet you got at least a dozen propositions."

"Two dozen," Lisa said sarcastically. "And yours was

the most distasteful of all!'' She jerked the car door open and got inside, fumbling to insert her key into the ignition.

The man leaned his hands against the door as he spoke through the window. ''You know, a come-on act like you performed tonight while you were dancing with all those men can be dangerous. You could lay yourself open to the wrong sort. You're beautiful, my little mermaid, and you aren't likely to ever have trouble attracting a man, but do you really need so many at once? Don't you think you might get in over your head that way?''

''I'm a good swimmer,'' Lisa retorted, with more anger than she'd ever felt toward another human being in her entire twenty-five years. ''I'm a mermaid, remember?''

He nodded somberly. ''Still, even a mermaid might have problems if she gets into water that's too deep.'' He removed his hands from the door as she started the car and took a step backward. ''Don't forget to have that flat tire fixed as soon as possible. No sense tempting fate.''

Chapter Two

It's a crazy idea, Lisa! If the man won't see you at his office, what makes you think he'll talk to you at his ranch?'' Veronica Wallace sneezed violently, grabbed a tissue and blew her nose. Her short brown hair was dull and limp, her face puffy, her nose red and the thick blue robe she wore was meant for winter weather, not a day in May. "Darn it! Why did I have to catch this miserable cold?" she asked. Not expecting an answer, she returned to the subject at hand. "I wish I'd never told you about Neugent's donation. He may get so mad at you for bothering him that it gets me fired. After all, Mr. Gillis gave us strict orders to keep it secret and besides that, he'd be furious if he knew I'd told you where Neugent's ranch is. I never dreamed you'd jump on all this like a dog worrying a bone.'' She hunched forward and sneezed again.

"Don't be silly!" Lisa chided, dismissing her friend's concern. "I won't say how I learned about it. Besides, there's no story at all if Neugent refuses the interview, so the whole thing will stay a secret if he won't talk to me. But a million dollars to establish a camp for abused and troubled kids donated by an ex–football star is a great human interest story, Roni! I have to try to get it, don't you see? My getting that job with *Today's Journal* depends on whether I can deliver this story. Here, drink this. It'll make you feel better." She set a mug filled with a mixture of steaming-hot water, honey and lemon juice on the kitchen bar.

Roni groaned. "Nothing's going to make me feel better if I lose my job. Besides, what if you get off into the wilds somewhere and that clunker you call a car breaks down or you have another flat? You might not find such an eager rescuer way out in the boondocks."

"I'll get my tire fixed before I go. Anyway, even if something did happen, I couldn't possibly meet up with another obnoxious boor like that!" Last night when she had returned home, Lisa had favored Roni with a blow-by-blow account of all that had happened. It had helped to be able to tell someone about it. She had gotten some of the poisonous rage out of her system, but this morning her blood pressure still rose whenever she remembered the man she had encountered. "Now, about today," she persisted, eager to get back to the discussion that interested her. "It's only a couple of hours' drive up there

. . . three at the most. I'll be back before dark or soon after, so stop worrying. Everything will be fine."

"Yeah," Roni said glumly. "I'll bet that's what Marie Antoinette said right up to the bitter end. Only in this case, it's *my* neck you're sticking out! Anybody with Neugent's kind of money to give the foundation has the power to have my head lopped off for this, Lisa. Please, just drop the whole thing. There must be a thousand other subjects you can write about!"

"True, but this is the one *Today's Journal* wants and I need that job, Roni! Otherwise I'll have to start pounding the pavement looking for some other kind of regular job. You know as well as I do I can't make it after you move out on the income I've been earning. I have to have a more dependable source of income and that's the long and short of it! But honestly, I swear I won't tell Neugent how I found out about his donation. And if I don't tell him, how can he possibly get you fired if he doesn't even know you exist?"

"Gillis will conduct an inquisition. He warned us not to talk to the press," she said, adding bitterly, "How was I to know I couldn't speak freely in my own home?"

Lisa gave her an impulsive hug. "I keep telling you, you're worrying over nothing. Now wish me luck before I go!"

"I wish you luck all right. I wish me luck, too . . . that I still have a job come Monday morning. Otherwise Jack's going to have to marry me sooner than he thinks so I can keep up the habit of eating."

Lisa laughed at her friend's gloomy forebodings and

went toward her bedroom to dress. It was unusual for Roni to be pessimistic and Lisa assumed it must be the bad cold that had her spirits so low. Normally, there was no one more adventurous and confident. She was the one who'd dared to drop a wad of chewing gum in old man Green's toupee during history class back when they were both students at UCLA; she was also the one who'd met her fiancé by bribing him with the offer of a home-cooked dinner when, as a patrolman, he had stopped her for speeding.

As she dressed for her trip in a neat apricot linen suit she had sewn herself, Lisa chuckled, recalling the evening six months ago when Roni had rushed in and exclaimed, "Quick! Cook something gourmet! It's either that or I'll go to jail!" Roni—fun-loving, risk-taking Roni—could scarcely boil an egg and she often got herself into messes because of a tendency to speak before thinking. Still, Jack Tilton had quickly become enthralled with her quicksilver, fun-loving personality, and it didn't seem to matter to him one whit that she couldn't cook. He had definite plans to marry her at Christmas.

When he did, Lisa knew that she was going to be in for a very lonely time. The two girls had been roommates since college. All the same, she was happy for Roni. There was no one like her and Jack was so obviously besotted over her that Lisa could only be glad for the both of them. Wistfully, she hoped that someday she would meet a man who would love her as much as Jack loved Roni. Certainly she had struck out where Kevin was concerned.

Lisa put Kevin and Roni both out of her mind as she left

the apartment and drove toward Santa Monica's water-front. Her thoughts flew ahead of her as she passed Lincoln Park with its eucalyptus and palm trees, and even when she reached Ocean Avenue she was more intent on her thoughts than she was on the enticing view of the bay. She had a sneaking suspicion that her trip was going to be a complete waste of time and inside she felt a little uneasy about tracking a man to his ranch when he had already made it patently clear that he had no desire to speak to her. Still, if she wanted to be known as a serious journalist, she had to develop the necessary thick skin and pursue her quarry until she caught him. Journalists worth their salt never gave up and her ambition was to one day be counted among the best.

As was always the case, traffic was heavy along the narrow stretch of coastal highway that led to Malibu. The blue Pacific bordered one side of the highway; steep cliffs and buildings clinging to them lined the other.

The magnificent beachfront homes of film stars and other wealthy Malibu residents finally came into view, and a few minutes later, as she reached the outskirts of the community, traffic began to thin.

The drive was unremarkable except for the lovely scenery of both sea and green, mountainous terrain; Lisa noticed little, preoccupied as she was with her thoughts, until, just past Ventura with its walnut trees and orange groves, she noticed clouds slowly building to the west, over the ocean.

By the time she approached Santa Barbara, the clouds were looking far more ominous. Lisa looked out beyond the picturesque harbor and the Channel Islands, now

watching the sky with a bit of anxiety. She hated the idea
of being caught in a rainstorm, but she'd already come too
far to turn back now.

Determined, she kept driving, all the while fervently
hoping the rain would hold off until tonight after she was
back home. But a few miles past Santa Barbara, the sky
turned more threatening still. Whiteness tinged with blue
turned to pale-gray and finally to charcoal. She didn't like
the angry look of them at all and, growing more uneasy by
the moment, began to genuinely regret having come on
what was probably a fool's errand anyway.

At Gaviota she left Pacific Coast Highway and turned
north. Once across the Gaviota Pass she began looking for
a likely place to stop and ask directions. She knew the
Neugent ranch was somewhere nearby, before the village
of Solvang. Fenced grazing land lined both sides of the
road and in the distance was the hazy blue outline of the
San Rafael Mountains and the denser blue-greens of the
surrounding forests.

A few minutes later she spotted a man locking a gate at
a private road and she stopped and asked, "Can you tell
me how to get to Anthony Neugent's ranch?"

"Sure." The man gave her the directions readily
enough, ending, "You can't miss it. The gate is a large
white metal one."

"Thanks," Lisa said, smiling. "Thanks a lot."

The man peered up at the rapidly darkening sky.
"Better get there quick as you can, young lady. Looks like
we're in for some rain."

Fortunately, the storm held off. As Lisa bumped down
the ill-tended country road a few minutes later, it suddenly

occurred to her that Anthony Neugent might not actually be at his ranch, despite what she'd overheard his secretary tell a telephone caller. If he wasn't there, then she was going to have to drive back to the city through a rainstorm all for nothing, because there was no longer any doubt in her mind that it would catch her. It was only a question of when.

At last she spied the tall white gate. With a sense of relief that was entirely unjustified since she was both unexpected and uninvited, Lisa drove through and rounded the curve of the gravel driveway. On a rise some distance ahead, she saw a rustic wooden cabin secluded behind a shelter of walnut and evergreen trees. Beyond the trees stretched barbed-wire fences and pastureland; off to the left was a barn and pens; to the right more grazing land rose and dipped over the gently rolling earth.

Lisa was a little surprised at the smallness and simplicity of the house itself. For a ranch belonging to a millionaire, the little cabin bore scant resemblance to the grand affair she'd expected to find, although as she parked her car she had to admit to herself that it appealed to her very much. A verandahlike porch surrounded the house on the three sides she could see and the front steps were guarded by two very old wagon wheels. A stone chimney rose at one end of the house, and all in all, there was a snug coziness about it that quietly bespoke unpretentious comfort and a slow-paced, relaxed mode of living.

As Lisa got out of her car, tired, anxious about the impending storm and unsure of what her welcome might be by the thus far unapproachable and enigmatic Mr. Neugent, she noticed a car just to the edge of the trees on the right side of the cabin. It was a '67 Mustang and its hood was raised. She could see a man's long, blue-jeaned legs in front of it. The rest of him was concealed by the hood.

Particles of loose soil imbedded in her slingback heels as Lisa made her way across the uneven ground toward the person tinkering with the inner workings of the car. Her shoes had definitely not been made for such rough terrain, she thought in frustration. For that matter, her suit was out of place here as well, but when she'd dressed this morning it had seemed important to present as neat and business-like an appearance as possible. Now, however, she thought perhaps it had been a mistake. She looked absurdly out of place in these surroundings and she knew it.

She was near the blue Mustang now, and though he surely must have heard her car coming up the drive, the man working beneath the hood still had not bothered to look up. She could see now that the top half of his body was bare. His head was bent, so that she couldn't see it, but his sun-browned back was visible. Perspiration gleamed on the skin and Lisa could see muscles playing, rippling and undulating like tall grass rolling in a field on a breezy day.

"Excuse me," Lisa spoke firmly when it was at last apparent to her that he wasn't going to emerge from beneath the hood without prompting.

Slowly, arms, hands, then head withdrew from the hidden dark recesses beneath the shade of the hood and the man straightened. He was tall, extraordinarily tall, and his hair was as dark as the grease that stained his hands. He reached toward a back pocket, pulled out a rag and began wiping his hands at the same time he turned his face toward Lisa.

Their gazes collided, and if lighting had struck, Lisa couldn't have been more dumbfounded or dismayed. Her heart literally stopped for an instant and when it resumed its intended function, it tattooed a rapid beat within her breast while her nerve endings tingled with alarm. She actually closed her eyes, as though they might be playing tricks on her, but when she opened them again they still gave the same mute evidence as before. The man who was now confronting her was the same man who had changed her tire last night, the very one who had so annoyed her at the party. It wasn't possible, and yet there he was, against all logic, reason or circumstantial odds.

The man seemed as astonished as she was. His dark eyes widened in obvious amazement, but then they narrowed thoughtfully as he eyed her. Lisa had the distinct impression that he was no more pleased to see her than she was to see him.

Although the silence couldn't have lasted longer than a minute at most, it seemed to stretch endlessly. The piercing intensity of his gaze intimidated Lisa and her own gaze skittered away, only to land on that wide, naked chest. Black hair curled down the center of it to trail away at the center of the waistband of his faded jeans. His body, the bare chest, the long legs with the powerful thighs in the tight-fitting jeans, his very stance, with his feet planted widely apart, exuded a potent, male sexuality and the sight of it brought an unfamiliar flutter to Lisa's stomach. She swallowed with difficulty and nervously lifted her gaze once more to his face.

While she was still trying to find her voice, the man jolted the strange, prestorm silence by slamming down the hood of the car. Swiftly he turned toward her once more and his voice was sharp and stabbing as it cut into her frantic, confused thoughts. "You've got a hell of a nerve following me here!"

His words wiped away the nervousness. Lisa bristled and her body went stiff and erect as she glared at him with the most intense dislike she'd ever felt toward another human being. "You've got to be kidding!" she retorted scathingly. "I wouldn't waste my time following you anywhere if you were the Pied Piper himself! I'm looking for the owner here. I presume," she said derisively as her eyes flickered scornfully down to his grease-stained hands, "that he's your employer. What were you doing last night," she added, "playing Mr. Bigshot driving his Porsche?"

The man's brow crinkled as he frowned and Lisa felt pleased that the taunt had hit home. He'd had it coming. She'd never met a more aggravating man in her life! With a haughty nod, Lisa concluded their discussion. "If you'll excuse me, I'll go on to the house. My business here is with Mr. Neugent, not you."

She had covered half the distance between the man and the porch before she heard him laugh, a loud, rumbling, hearty laugh that seemed to fill the very air.

The sound paralyzed Lisa. She stopped and for a long moment was incapable of moving. She scarcely even breathed as a cold chill filled her with foreboding. Why hadn't she guessed sooner? The powerful physique, the solid muscles . . . the classic football player build. Slowly, with the utmost reluctance, she turned to face him again and the indecent amusement in his eyes warned her that her suspicion was justified.

All the color drained from her face. "You're not . . ." She was floundering, but she couldn't seem to help herself. "You can't possibly be . . ." Words failed and she fell silent, her vocal cords as dead as her suddenly lifeless arms and legs.

He covered the yards between them in a few short strides. A wide grin stretched across his face as he loomed above her, huge, physically commanding and altogether intimidating. He gave an elaborate bow, as though he were meeting the queen, and could scarcely conceal his laughter as he said, "Anthony Neugent. At least that's what my driver's license says."

By slow degrees, feeling returned to Lisa's body and with it, excruciating embarrassment. Her color came back, burning hot, and unconsciously she lifted a hand to one feverish cheek. She hadn't thought she had much of a chance of convincing Neugent to submit to an interview before they met and now she was sure of it. After the things she'd said, the way she had behaved toward this man, she had about as much chance of getting her story now as she did of becoming the first woman president of the country.

The amusement he'd just had at her expense fizzled away. Anthony Neugent was no longer laughing as he looked at her with a stern expression. "I'd like an answer to my question. What are you doing here?'' He cocked his head to one side and squinted his eyes at her. "Do mermaids always follow men around when they get to dry land?'' It was a dig, a rhetorical question, and he went on without waiting for an answer. "And speaking of that subject''—he waved a hand toward her in a gesture of disapproval—"if you're trying to impress me by a prim and proper guise, you've missed the mark. I've seen your sexy dress of the sea, remember? I much prefer it to this staid schoolmarm outfit you're wearing.''

Lisa couldn't help retorting, "But last night I was dressed entirely too suggestively to suit you. Obviously I can't possibly please you, no matter what I wear.''

"Could be,'' he said unhelpfully. "Could be, at that. So, Miss Mermaid, are you ever going to tell me what you're doing here or is this a guessing game?'' He glanced up at the threatening sky before returning his gaze to Lisa's face. "Either way, you better hurry. The sky's about to open up.''

Lisa sucked in a ragged breath. Things were being far more difficult than she had expected. Even the weather refused to cooperate! She took one more short glimpse of Anthony Neugent's impatient face and plunged. After all, what could she lose? "My name is Lisa Knight and I came to . . .'' She stopped abruptly at the expression on his face. Anger flashed from his eyes and at that exact same instant the heavy deluge began.

"Get off my property,'' he ordered without any attempt to soften his words.

Lisa was shocked at the sudden change in him. She'd

been prepared for his displeasure and maybe even a bit of curt unfriendliness, but not this frightening hostility.

They were both getting soaked as they stood facing each other in the rain, and while Lisa was aware of a growing chill, she wasn't quite ready to give up. "Oh, now come," she cajoled. "You don't even know yet why I want to talk to you."

"I know enough." His voice was gruff. "You're a reporter. You're the one who's been calling my office all week. Well, it's true, I don't know what it's all about and what's more, I don't give the least little damn! I don't talk to the press."

"You're being unreasonable!" Lisa practically had to shout over the downpour. By now her hair and clothes clung to her body, limp and soggy, and Neugent's jeans were molded around his legs as though he'd been poured into them. "I want to write a magazine article about your generous donation to the Cameron Children's Foundation for troubled youth. It's a fine thing you did and because you're already popular and well-known from your football days, it'll make a wonderful story and the public will love it! Can't you see what good publicity it would be for you?"

"I don't need any publicity, good or otherwise," Neugent said so savagely that without even thinking, Lisa took a cautious step backward. "And I want nothing to do with you and your kind. I was sure my secretary had made that clear to you. Now kindly do us both a favor and get off my land before I have to throw you off!" He took a threatening step toward her.

Lisa backed away another step. "All right," she said, furious with herself to discover she was trembling. "You win. I'll go. But if I do, you won't win entirely. I really need this assignment, and if you won't cooperate and give me an interview, I'll have no choice but to go ahead with my article without you, using old material from press clippings to flesh out the story. If I have to do that, I can guarantee the story won't be nearly as flattering as it might otherwise have been."

Tony was so incensed by her threat that he automatically balled his fists into the lethal weapons they were. His entire body tensed for battle before logic reasserted itself when he saw her fear of him. This was a woman . . . a small slip of a woman. He could scarcely release his pent-up physical violence on her! Slowly, he uncurled his hands and his laugh was harsh and grating. "Don't worry," he sneered as he saw her fear, "I've never hit a woman in my life, even when they've deserved it, so you won't be the first. That won't prevent me from putting you off this place forcibly, though, if I have to do it. But before you go, maybe I'd better warn you about one thing. If you go ahead with your article without my permission, I'll sue you and your magazine for libel."

The girl's large green eyes widened. "How could you? You don't even know yet what it would say. You can't know you'd find anything libelous in it!"

Tony shrugged and brushed an arm across his wet face. "It doesn't matter. My lawyer will find something, anything, and we'll see you in court. I don't care whether I win or lose, but it ought to tie you up for a while so that no one else will be wanting your byline until the case gets settled.''

"Why, that's blackmail!'' she sputtered.

Tony's mouth twisted into a grim smile. "I prefer to call it a friendly little piece of advice, but you're the writer, of course. Call it whatever you like.''

Her shoulders went back and her chin went up. She looked like a sparrow defying an eagle and something deep within Tony grudgingly respected that.

"I don't scare as easily as that!'' she told him. "We do still have free press in this country, in case you've forgotten.''

"Oh, I haven't forgotten,'' he said bitterly. "You leeches and bloodsuckers hide behind the First Amendment while you destroy the lives of innocent people in the name of the public's right to know. You dig, endlessly dig, until you find something a person would rather forget and live down, then smear it across newspapers and magazines or TV screens to titillate the masses with a scandal until you've done all the damage you can for the moment to that one individual, and then you move on to the next poor, hapless victim. You're all scum of the earth and not a one of you knows the definition of the word *compassion*. Go on,'' he ended with suppressed fury, "go write your story, but remember what I said because I meant it!''

Not trusting himself to stand there any longer, Tony left her in the pouring rain and went quickly toward the porch. He mounted the steps two at a time and, without even looking back to make sure she was leaving, opened the door and went inside.

Only when the door was safely shut and the girl could not possibly see him, was there any evidence of the true depths of the wild fury that shook him. Leaning one arm across the door, Tony bent his wet head to rest upon it while he sucked in one deep, shuddering breath after another in an effort to still the rage that assaulted his entire body.

God, how he detested journalists! He lifted his head, pulled his arm back from the door and slammed his fist into it. Damn them all and this one in particular! Hadn't he had enough unpleasant dealings with the press in the past without having to endure still more? What did they want out of him . . . his blood? His very life? He supposed so. No matter how they'd embarrassed or humiliated him in print, he'd held on, never buckling under, not like some who simply hadn't had the stamina to stand up under such vicious attacks.

He thought sadly of Danny Milstead, a former teammate and his closest friend eight years ago. Danny had been one of those who hadn't been able to hang on. He'd made the mistake once of being human, all too tragically human, and the press had crucified him for it. A power-horse on the playing field, he'd discovered how helpless he was against their relentless onslaught. The press was an enormous, nameless, faceless giant, a shadow that loomed cruelly over every public figure, always at the ready to pounce when one was least able to fight back. Even David of biblical days could not have slain a shadowy Goliath such as the modern-day press.

But once in a while one could get in a lucky punch at one little piece of the shadow. Tony had done it once. Of course, it had only resulted in even more problems and the pen had continued to prove its might, but he recalled with satisfaction the ugly black eye with which he'd gifted that certain detested reporter. However, a woman was different.

Tony frowned. A beautiful woman, at that. Last evening when he'd happened upon her on that canyon road, dressed in that alluring costume, he'd been absolutely staggered by an unreasonable attraction to her. He'd wanted very much to get to know her, but a chance encounter on the side of the road at dusk had been an impossible situation. There had been no way to attempt to set up a future meeting without alarming her, so when he'd seen her later at the party, he had at once been delighted at the chance to become acquainted under more normal circumstances. Only two things had been wrong with that: she hadn't been disposed to be friendly and he'd been so ridiculously jealous of other men seeing her dressed so skimpily, not to mention dancing with her, that he hadn't been very diplomatic in the things he'd said to her.

To this minute he couldn't understand or explain to himself why he'd been interested in her. After all, he was used to beautiful women. He'd dated a few of the most gorgeous women in Hollywood, a circumstance that had taught him a valuable-enough lesson about the treachery of beautiful women. Though nowadays he steered clear of any involvement with actresses, he still went out with extremely good-looking women, but he maintained a strict guard on his emotions. So why had this woman gotten through the barrier?

But today when he'd seen her standing in his driveway, all cool and proper, yet with what he'd thought was outrageous audacity to follow him here after their encounter at the party, he had been far from pleased. He never brought any women to his ranch; this was his special retreat from the world. Besides, he'd been furious to think she was that forward. It went against what he liked in any woman. For the most part, Tony approved of the confidence and independence of the modern woman, but when it came to the age-old man/woman chase, he wanted to do the pursuing. Especially when they'd never even been introduced! But then, when she'd said her name, it had completely shattered the attraction he'd originally felt toward her. He had recognized her name at once. All week long his secretary had been giving him messages that a journalist by that name was trying to reach him. That she would actually dare to invade his hideaway was utterly unforgivable.

The rain continued to thunder down upon the roof and gradually Tony calmed down enough to be aware of it. He was also aware that he was soaking wet and cold. He went down the hall to the bathroom, grabbed a thick towel and, rubbing it across his face and hair, retraced his steps back to the living room and went into the kitchen to put a kettle of water on to boil. Coffee was what he needed.

Tony left the water to boil and went toward his bedroom to get dry clothes.

Wet, cold and shivering, Lisa huddled miserably inside the car. She had to calm down and stop trembling before she could dare drive away in this storm. The rain fell with such violence that she could scarcely see through the window and what she did see was nothing but a gray blur.

She glanced toward the snug, inviting cabin nestled behind the trees. Lights glimmered warmly from its windows, seeming to dance through the rain. Lisa felt near tears as she gazed at it. Oh, to be dry and warm and out of the storm, which was pounding more viciously by the minute.

What bad luck that Anthony Neugent had turned out to be the same man she'd met last night! Even worse, that he had become so hostile and angry when he'd learned who she was. She had half expected to have her request for an interview turned down summarily, but in a decent, calm, civilized way. The last thing she had expected was for him to turn into a crazy man just because she was a journalist. Heavens, you'd think she had some sort of highly contagious disease! When he'd doubled his fists and taken that step toward her, she had honestly feared for her safety for a moment. As a matter of fact, she still wasn't entirely convinced he would not harm her, particularly if she didn't hurry up and make a move to get off his property.

Grimacing, Lisa started the car and as she peered out into the gloom of the solid gray sheet of rain, her spirits dropped even lower. It looked like the kind of storm that could go on for hours, maybe even all through the night. It was going to be a long and difficult drive back home. If only she had never come in the first place!

She turned the car around and started slowly down the drive. It was a long driveway, probably close to a quarter of a mile between the cabin and the gate. The land sloped downward and the car gained momentum of its own accord.

Lisa was a tense bundle of nerves. She was still shaken by the scene with Anthony Neugent and now she was concerned with the weather. The windshield wipers were working at full speed, but she could scarcely see anything beyond the downpour.

She made up her mind that once she was off Neugent's property she would stop on the side of the road and wait out the storm, or at least the worst of it. This was impossible driving weather and it would be foolish to attempt it when she could barely see ahead of her.

The huge arc above the gate loomed up out of the solid gray sheet. Only a few more yards and she would be through it.

At that moment, Lisa heard a loud thud. It was followed at once by a violent vibration of the car. The car veered to the right, the steering wheel no longer operable, and before she could even catch her breath, much less figure out what was happening, incredibly, the car tipped sideways!

About to slip on his shirt, Tony stood transfixed at his bedroom window. The girl's car had just gone out of control! He could scarcely believe the evidence of his eyes as it leaned to one side as though it were going to flip over. Then, miraculously, it righted itself before swerving off the drive and plowing down a small grassy slope, where it came to a jolting, abrupt stop.

Tony's heart thudded wildly as he tossed aside the shirt

and ran through the house. Outside he wasn't even aware of the fierce rain that pelted down on him as he raced down the drive like a madman. His anxiety about whether she'd been injured was all-consuming. Adrenaline sped through his veins, propelling him even faster than the best time he'd ever run before on a football field.

Lisa was still somewhat dazed when the car door was wrenched open. She was trembling and cold and when she looked up into Anthony Neugent's face and saw the anxiety there, the real reason for it didn't immediately penetrate her mind.

"I'm sorry," she said dully. "I meant to leave. I . . . I just don't know what happened."

"Forget it!" His voice was rough as he reached for her. "Are you all right? Are you hurt anywhere?"

"I don't think so," Lisa said slowly, for the first time giving the matter consideration.

Neugent caught her arm in his hand and assisted her out of the car. His dark eyes seemed to burn her face as he gazed down at her and then, incredibly, he pulled her into his arms against his bare chest. Only then did Lisa feel the trembling within him that matched her own.

Strangely, it felt wonderfully warm and safe there despite the pouring rain, despite the heated words they had exchanged only moments ago. Giving in to the weakness that had come over her, Lisa bent her head and rested it against his shoulder.

After a time they both grew calmer and steadier. Neugent released her and the gentle concern he had exhibited for her welfare was gone. Both his demeanor and his words were emotionless. "You'll simply have to stay here until the storm's over and I can check on your car." He glanced down at her feet and frowned. "Better take those high heels off. You'll never make it uphill to the cabin wearing them. The ground's too slippery."

Knowing how unwelcome she was, Lisa didn't move. It was all simply more than she could bear. Tears were hot behind her eyelids and she fought them fiercely. She blinked her eyes and swallowed painfully. If she broke down and cried, it would be the clincher, the absolute clincher, topping everything else.

Anthony Neugent cursed softly beneath his breath. "I've never met a more exasperating woman in my life! Now are you going to go up to the cabin under your own steam or do I have to carry you there myself?"

"You don't want me here," Lisa said in a muffled voice.

"No, I'm not going to pretend that I do," he said with devastating honesty. "But it looks like I'm stuck with you all the same, just as you're stuck with me. Now let's quit wasting time. We don't need to stand around out here in the rain and catch pneumonia. You go on up to the cabin while I check on some things in the barn first. Or do you need me to help you?" His eyes narrowed. "Do you have an injury you didn't tell me about?"

Lisa shook her head. "No. I'm fine and I can walk by myself." Because she seemed to have no other choice, she bent to remove her shoes and, while Neugent stood there watching, began walking through the mud and the rain back toward the cabin.

When she reached it, she climbed the porch steps, but at the door she hesitated. She had the strangest sensation that somehow just by crossing that threshold, she was also crossing over a new threshold in her own life, after which she would never again be the same.

Chapter Three

*T*ony watched her go and then he closed the car door and headed toward the barn. One of his horses was there with a sprain.

Inside the snug, dry warmth of the barn, he checked to see that the mare had enough hay and water and then, taking his time, unwrapped her leg, rubbed some liniment on the swelling and put a fresh bandage around it. "You're coming along fine, baby," Tony murmured. He stood up and gave an affectionate pat on her flank. "By tomorrow when the storm is over you ought to be out in the pasture prancing around and feeling good as new."

With nothing remaining to do, yet filled with an odd reluctance to return to the cabin and the girl who was there, Tony stood at the opened barn door. The sky was dark, almost like night, although it was still only midafternoon. The distant hills were completely enshrouded by the blue-gray sheet of rain. He hoped this wasn't going to be one of those Pacific storms that went on for days, saturating the hills until there were damaging mudslides. His own property here was fairly safe because it was on gently sloping terrain rather than a steep hillside and his Malibu beach house ought to be all right, too, if the storm had hit there also. Unless the waves had gone crazy, of course. But some of his friends and neighbors who had hillside homes in either place might not be so fortunate. And if the roads went out, he might be stuck here for days. With her.

Tony grimaced, scarcely understanding himself. He'd been scared out of his wits when he'd thought Lisa Knight might be injured. When he'd pulled her into his arms, it had seemed like a natural thing to do, something anyone would do after someone they cared about had been in danger. He could still feel the softness of her hair against his bare skin. All the same, now, with a little distance between them and the knowledge that she was all right, his original anger and resentment of her had returned. To think that he of all people had to play host to a reporter! It might have been funny, but cold, wet and annoyed, Tony didn't find much humor in the irony of it. Yet standing here brooding about it wasn't going to change the situation. Besides, it was getting colder by the minute and he was still soaking wet.

When he went into the cabin, he saw the girl standing in the kitchen next to the table. Her back was to him and her head was bent. Her shoulders drooped and there was an unmistakable aura of abject misery about her. Her wet, wrinkled clothes clung to her like clammy fingers and her hair hung in dark, dripping clumps down her back. While he watched he saw her shiver with a chill and rub her arms with her hands. Certainly she didn't look very self-confident or threatening just now. She also bore no resemblance to the sex goddess she'd been last night. She simply looked like a pitiful lost soul who was tired, cold, probably hungry and desperately unhappy.

Tony's heart softened. She appeared overwhelmed by the unfortunate circumstances that for the time being forced her to remain here where she knew she wasn't wanted. For an instant, he forgot everything except a desire to make things easy for her. He actually took a step forward, feeling an urge to touch her for the simple human warmth of it, but abruptly he checked himself. Had he gone crazy? he wondered. He'd better never forget what she really was—a vulture, something lower than a rattlesnake . . . in fact, a journalist.

He must have made some sound because she whirled around to face him, her eyes large and dark with anxiety. "I turned off your stove burner," she said defensively, as though he might condemn her for having taken the liberty. "The kettle was singing."

Tony nodded. "I forgot about it. I'd put it on to make coffee and when I went to the bedroom to change, I happened to look out the window and see your car going out of control." His voice and manner roughened as he recalled the horror that had filled him at the sight. To cover it, his gaze flickered impersonally over her. "We both need to get out of these wet clothes. Come with me."

Her look was wary, untrusting, and for a moment she

didn't move. Tony lost his patience. "Maybe you want to stay wet and cold?" he sneered.

She shook her head and took a tentative step in his direction. Tony turned and went down the hall, not bothering to see whether she followed him or not.

In his bedroom, he flung open the closet door, grabbed a brown velour robe and, turning to find her in the doorway with a nervous expression on her face, tossed it angrily in her direction. "Don't worry," he snapped in a grating voice that unmistakably illustrated the irritation he was feeling. "You're safe enough. You're not the kind of woman I invite into my bedroom for fun and games. I'd as soon invite a tiger in as an equally destructive, cold-hearted reporter!"

He saw her eyes widen and then quickly shutter as her lashes swept down. He hadn't been able to read the emotion in them, whether it was fear, resentment, relief or something else altogether. Not that it mattered. Why should he care what this girl thought, anyway? After the storm was over and something was done about her car, he'd never see her again.

As though drawing a mask over her face, Lisa Knight's expression went carefully blank. He had thought his comments might incite her into sparring with him, and, strangely, he felt a little disappointed when that didn't happen.

"If you'll tell me where I can change, I would appreciate it," she said in a bland voice.

"The bathroom's down the hall," he informed her. "You'd better get a hot bath to warm you up. You're still trembling. There's a spare bedroom across the hall if you

care to use it, too." He frowned thoughtfully as his gaze
flickered over her hopelessly crumpled jacket and skirt.
"Can your clothes be put in the dryer?" At her nod, he
added, "Fine. You can dry them as soon as you're
changed. Now, if you'll kindly go away, I'd like to get out
of my soaking clothes, too."

He reached for the belt buckle at his waist and tugged at
it. The girl saw his action and, looking suddenly frantic,
bolted from the door. When he heard the bathroom door
slam, Tony laughed grimly. Score one for the victim.

No matter how many reassurances Anthony Neugent
might offer about not being interested in fun and games
with a coldhearted reporter, Lisa did not so much as
remove her jacket until she was certain the bathroom door
was securely locked. He was a man and a stranger and
that, in her book, was enough. The fact that he frankly
disliked her altered nothing, except to make her even more
wary. More than once since their first meeting on the side
of the road last night, he had looked at her the way a man
looks at a woman when he's interested. He might despise
her character, her work and anything else he could think
of, but he was not indifferent to her physically.

She ran hot water into the tub and began undressing.
Her teeth were chattering badly by the time her icy fingers
peeled off her wet, clinging panty hose and saturated bra.
When she climbed into the bathtub, she could hear the rain
pounding relentlessly on the roof, a forceful reminder that
she was imprisoned here on this remote ranch with a man
who had some kind of maniacal hatred of journalists.
What a predicament she had landed herself in!

She simply wasn't cut out for this sort of excitement. Perhaps, she mused as she allowed her body to sink beneath the warm cover of the water, she should reassess her career ambitions. Writing was a more dangerous profession than she had imagined. If she was smart, she'd go to the unemployment office first thing next week and seek the sheltering safety of an office job where life was safe and predictable each day, and forget about the job at *Today's Journal*.

Lisa remained behind the locked bathroom door as long as she dared, but after a long time she realized how silly that was and how stupid she would appear to her grudging host if she didn't emerge within a reasonable time. She could hardly spend the rest of her life locked up here. She had to get her clothes dried and her car running so that she could leave—provided, of course, the storm had let up by then, which seemed more and more doubtful by the minute.

She combed her wet hair and let it hang loose over the collar of the massive robe. The hem of it trailed the floor and while she rolled the sleeves so that her hands were free, she couldn't help but think how strange it felt to be wearing such a personal item belonging to a man she had scarcely met. An unaccustomed shyness stole over Lisa as she at last left the privacy of the bathroom and went barefoot down the hall, carrying her bundle of wet clothing.

She found her host in the kitchen, neatly dressed in fresh, dry jeans and a white western-style shirt that molded itself to his huge shoulders. He was standing near the window, gazing out at the rain.

"Is it slowing down any at all?" she asked quietly.

He turned from the window to look at her, but his glance was casual and disinterested, which went a long way toward easing the tension within her.

"Doesn't look like it," he replied. He stepped toward a door and opened it. "The dryer's in here. Just put your shoes anywhere," he added as he saw them dangling from her fingers. "There's not a whole lot we can do for them."

Lisa went past him into the small utility room. She opened the dryer and began stuffing her clothes into it while Neugent called from the kitchen, "Want some coffee?"

"Please," she answered. Lisa closed the dryer door, set the timer and went back into the kitchen.

"Have a seat." He indicated the table while he poured two mugs of coffee.

Lisa sat down. "Do you have any idea what's wrong with my car?"

Neugent shrugged as he replaced the coffeepot on the stove. "I'm not sure. I know you're anxious about it, but there's not really anything we can do except wait until the rain stops and then see to it."

A small silence fell as Tony carried the mugs of coffee to the table. Swallowing her concern over her car, Lisa glanced around at her surroundings for the first time. When she'd been in here earlier she'd been too upset and cold to notice anything. Now she saw that the kitchen, though small, was well arranged. Pine cabinets and paneling gave it a homey touch. The living room, which opened off the kitchen through a dividing bar, also had the same paneling. A rock fireplace took up one end of the room. A comfortable tweed sofa and matching chair were arranged to face the fireplace. A small portable TV set rested on one end of the bar where it could easily be turned toward the living room or the kitchen. There was nothing fancy about the place at all, just solid comfort, and yet it appealed to her.

"You have a nice place here," she said as Neugent set her coffee before her.

He sat down opposite her and, while she stirred sugar into her cup, said, "Yeah, I think so, too, considering I'd never built anything before."

"You built it yourself?" she asked, surprised.

For the first time, Anthony Neugent smiled quite naturally, and Lisa was a little stunned at the transformation it made. It enhanced his rugged good looks as it wiped away the former surliness. "Sure," he replied, nodding. "Board by board, stone by stone, with a bit of help from some friends whenever there was a job requiring more than two hands. You look as though you don't believe me," he said accusingly. "What's the matter? Don't you think I'm strong enough to build a house?"

"Don't be absurd!" Lisa found herself laughing as her gaze swept over his massive frame. "You're probably strong enough to have built the pyramids all by yourself!" She shook her head and went on thoughtfully. "It's just that this place isn't exactly what I would have expected for someone like you. A wealthy man . . ."

His smile was instantly gone and he cut her off brusquely. "I didn't build it for show. I built it to enjoy."

Lisa raised her hands, signifying surrender. "I wasn't

criticizing," she said quickly. "I was just saying that it didn't fit my preconceived notions about the sort of house a millionaire would own, that's all. Do you spend a lot of time here?"

Neugent shrugged and took a sip of his coffee. "Not as much as I'd like. My business interests keep me pretty busy in the city."

She could easily understand that. He headed the Neugent Investment Corporation in Los Angeles and it handled a lot of big properties and investment plans. It had a sound reputation and Lisa had a feeling its success was almost entirely due to its shrewd owner. Besides having once played a fine game of football, this man also seemed to be an expert at playing the game of high finance.

"Do you run cattle?" she asked.

"Some Angus. Say, what're you trying to do?" he demanded suddenly. "Squeeze in your interview after all?" He slammed his coffee mug to the table.

Lisa swallowed hard. Lord, the man had a quick temper! "I was just trying to make conversation," she explained. "I'm sorry I'm being an imposition. Believe me, if I could get my car going right now I'd leave, storm or no storm. I don't enjoy being where I'm not wanted, no matter what you may think!" Her lower lip trembled, betraying her overwrought emotions, and she caught it between her teeth while she averted her head.

Silence fell heavily upon them and Lisa wished with all her heart that she had never heard of Anthony Neugent, much less made the dreadful mistake of coming here to find him.

Finally, Neugent broke the tense silence. "Maybe I was

a little rough on you just then,'' he said in a low voice. ''Sorry. Want some more coffee?'' he added as though to make amends.

Lisa nodded without looking at him and she heard his chair scrape as he got to his feet. When he came back with the coffeepot, he spoke again, casually. ''You were asking about my ranch. I've got several hundred acres and I love every inch of the place. It's where I unwind and leave the world behind.''

He was trying to make peace and Lisa knew it would be churlish as well as ungrateful for the shelter he was providing her if she didn't do her part to get on with polite conversation, too, no matter how difficult it was for the both of them.

''Do you have someone living here to take care of the place while you're away?'' she inquired.

''A neighboring rancher tends to things for me. It works out well for both of us.''

''Why do you hate reporters so much?'' she asked softly, unable to resist the question that was uppermost in her thoughts.

She saw a blood vessel pulsate at his temple and his large, strong fingers tightened around the coffee mug in front of him.

''I have my reasons,'' he stated flatly, ''but I'd rather not go into them.''

''We're not such a bad breed as you seem to think,'' Lisa said. ''Obviously you've had some bad encounters, but is it really fair of you to tar us all with the same brush?''

Tony's gaze was scornful and some deep anger burned

like smoking charcoals in his dark gaze. "I have yet," he said in a measured tone, "to meet one who had a conscience."

Lisa resented his blanket indictment. "It's quite clear," she said stiffly, "that you're utterly unreasonable on this subject."

"Very true," he surprised her by agreeing. "So it's probably wisest if we drop it, don't you think?"

"I think," she said, getting up from her chair, "that I'll check and see if my clothes are dry so that I can get dressed."

Sudden amusement lurked in his gaze. "That's too bad," he drawled. "My robe never looked better. A beautiful mermaid becomes it." His gaze fixed on the bare skin of her throat above the crisscross of the collar and lowered slowly to the curve of her breasts.

Not enjoying his amusement and growing hot and nervous beneath that gaze, Lisa pulled the robe tighter across her breasts, extremely conscious that beneath the brown folds she was naked. With more haste than grace, she turned abruptly and went out to the utility room to fetch her clothes, while, reverting to his earlier cruel baiting, Anthony Neugent laughed.

Tony had no qualms about making the girl uncomfortable. Offense was always better than defense and he was an expert at the game. Playing the offensive was challenging, exhilarating, giving power over one's destiny, and he certainly had no intention of letting one small female place him on the defensive.

While she locked herself into the bathroom a second

time, a fact that gave Tony a sort of perverse pleasure, he rinsed out the coffee mugs and peered out the window again. The rain showed no signs of slacking off. Short of getting out his car and driving her back to L.A. himself, which he had no intention of doing in this foul weather, he seemed to be stuck with his lovely adversary for a while longer. Surely the deluge would end soon and he'd have an opportunity to see what could be done about her car.

Meantime, though it was early, he might as well start supper, he decided. It would give him something to do with his restless energy and he'd also have it out of the way in case the rain stopped early enough for him to get outside to check her car.

He started browning meat in a Dutch oven and then began peeling potatoes. Lisa Knight had told him she needed the assignment of writing a story about him, yet her expensive clothes belied any need for money. The suit she had worn here was expertly tailored, the blouse silky and expensive-looking. She was a fool if she thought she could come here dressed like a million dollars and then expect him to fall for a hard-luck story. Tony knew the difference between cheap clothing and the best. He'd worn both kinds in his lifetime.

No, he thought as he stirred the meat, she was just like all other women . . . out to take a man for all he was worth. In this case she wanted his story, not his money. Probably such a beautiful, well-dressed woman had a generous man in her life who provided everything she needed and because she was bored and didn't have to make an honest living, she played at writing and getting into acting just to swell her ego. He imagined she got a great kick out of seeing her name in print. Most likely she hoped to see it one day on a list of movie credits, too. Like so many other women he'd met, she was a strikingly lovely, decorative butterfly, with too much time on her hands and nothing worthwhile to do with it. Tony had nothing but contempt for such women who could waste away much of a day tending to their flawless complexions, spending hours at the hairdressers, shopping for clothes and starving themselves so they could remain model slim. They were a brainless bunch of parasites!

Of course, he recalled angrily as he chopped an onion, he had learned the hard way about women. Young and enthralled when he'd met Carmen, he had blinded himself to the truth. But later, she had given him an education that he would never forget.

Tony put away his brooding thoughts when Lisa Knight rejoined him. Dressed in the rumpled skirt and blouse, barefoot and with her face scrubbed clean and her hair only half-dry and damply curling close to her head, she looked a great deal different from the impeccably polished, confident young woman who had approached him earlier. Now she looked like a teenager, innocent and cute rather than beautiful, and certainly not threatening.

Noting his expression, she wrinkled her nose. "Don't say it," she told him. "I realize how awful I look. You wouldn't happen to have an iron and ironing board handy, would you?"

He shook his head. "Sorry. I don't run to that much domesticity here. You don't look all *that* bad," he added kindly. "Only very young."

"Ummm. I wouldn't win any prizes for neatness,

either, though," she said with a grimace. "What's that heavenly smell?" She sniffed the air like someone savoring a fine wine.

"Stew. One of my specialties. Are you hungry?"

"Famished," she admitted. "Can I help?"

"You can set the table and open a package of biscuits while I make a salad, I suppose."

Lisa eyed him thoughtfully. "Do you happen to have flour, baking powder and milk?"

Tony nodded. "Why?"

"Instead of packaged biscuits, why don't I make some from scratch?"

Tony was surprised and his face frankly reflected it. "You know how to make homemade biscuits?"

Lisa laughed. "Is that so astonishing?"

"Pretty much so," he admitted. "I don't think I've met many women under fifty who bother to do things like that anymore."

"Don't be silly," Lisa chided. "It's no big deal."

An unspoken truce existed between the two of them as they worked together preparing their meal. They talked of nonvolatile subjects like food and travel and the ever-fascinating subject of the weather. Lisa kept to herself her growing alarm as the rain continued to pelt the cabin and the ground outside with ferocious intensity. It was getting later and later and she was becoming more anxious with every passing minute.

When they had finished their meal and were clearing the table, though, her anxiety spilled over as she paused to glance out the window. "It looks as though it's never going to end." Her voice quivered over the words.

"Maybe we ought to listen to a weather report," Tony said. He went to the bar and switched on the small radio that was beside the TV set.

A few minutes later, while Lisa washed and Tony dried the dishes, the report came. "The heavy rain is expected to continue throughout the night and perhaps into the morning. So far no major highways or bridges are out, but officials are keeping a close watch . . ."

Lisa heard no more. Without blinking, she stared in dismay at her hands in the sudsy dishwater. She couldn't bring herself to look at the man beside her.

"It seems," he said after a long silence, "that you'll have to stay the night."

She went pale and it was a moment before she found her voice and managed to speak. Still without looking at him, she ventured, "Surely there's a motel I can go to for the night? I could call a cab to come for me."

"In this weather?" Neugent looked at her with amazement. "Have you seen the road during the last half hour? It's beginning to flood. In a little while, if it keeps up like this, even a four-wheel drive would have trouble getting through."

"But I . . ." her throat tightened and at last she forced herself to meet his eyes. "I can't stay here all night!" She was horrified at the thought.

Tony shrugged indifferently. "Do whatever you please," he said. "You can sleep in your car or the barn for all I care. It's your decision." He tossed down the towel, strode out of the room and through the front door. The roar of the storm was loud, but then became diffused again as he closed the door behind him.

His unconcern infuriated Lisa. At the same time, perversely, it made her feel a little safer. If she had to spend the night here in this cabin alone with him, then it was infinitely better that he be apathetic about her presence, wasn't it?

She finished the remainder of the dishes alone while her thoughts chased around and around her dilemma. Spending the night in an isolated cabin with a total stranger was against every prudent rule there was. Yet what choice did she actually have? It wouldn't be any safer to set out walking in the night and through a storm. You had to weigh one evil against another and then go with the lesser of the two.

At last she opened the front door and went out onto the porch. Neugent sat in a redwood chair, feet propped up on the porch railing as he eyed the wild elements. Lisa's gaze followed his and she saw that just as he'd said, the public road beyond was already underwater as the rain poured down the sides of the surrounding hills. A small lake had formed at the foot of the drive from the runoff. The air was decidedly chilly and she wrapped her arms around herself.

"Well?" he asked at last without bothering to look at her. "You staying or going?"

"Staying, of course," she answered in a clipped tone. "What choice do I have? I can scarcely swim back to L.A."

He did look at her then and there was a devilish glint in his eyes. "No? I thought maybe you could, being a mermaid and all."

"I've had about enough of the mermaid subject, if you

don't mind," Lisa said in exasperation. "I'd like to forget last night, the stupid commercial and the ridiculous costume."

Neugent's feet came crashing down to the surface of the porch, and in a flash he was standing only a few inches from her. His grin was maddening. "You can forget it if you like," he teased, "but I have no intention of doing so. How many men can claim to have met a mermaid in the flesh?" He traced one large finger down her cheek, causing her skin to warm, and then he brushed her hair away from her neck as his thumb gently stroked the sensitive area there. "I think," he murmured softly as he came closer, "I'd like to find out how it feels to kiss one."

Lisa couldn't move. His eyes mesmerized her just before he closed them and claimed her lips.

It wasn't a passionate kiss. Rather it was one of experimentation, as though he were indeed kissing a creature from a different dimension. His lips were soft, unexpectedly gentle, sipping at hers, tasting, testing, teasing.

As abruptly as he had come to her, he released her and stepped away. "Actually," he said conversationally, as though nothing had just occurred, "I believe mortal women are better at kissing. Perhaps it's because they're more experienced."

Lisa was outraged. It was bad enough that he had taken the liberty without being invited, but to actually dare to criticize! She sucked in a breath and tried to control the fury that raged through her.

"You . . . you . . . I could kill you for that!" she sputtered.

He grinned cruelly. "What? The kiss . . . or because I didn't carry the thing further?"

"What are you?" she demanded scornfully. "Some sort of egotistical idiot who thinks every woman in the world is just waiting around for you to make love to her? Believe me, I can live very well without your unwelcome attentions. Let me tell you, Mr. Hotshot Neugent, your technique needs work!" With her head held high, she left him standing there and went back inside.

It was a half an hour before he came in and for a while they scrupulously avoided so much as looking at each other. Lisa sat on the sofa, flipping through a three-month-old *Time* while Tony switched on the television and sank into the easy chair.

Finally, Lisa knew she had to break the silence, much as it aggravated her to have to do it first. "Mr. Neugent?" He merely looked at her, forcing her to go on. "Do you mind if I use your phone? My roommate will be worried sick if I don't call to say I'm all right."

"Be my guest. One thing, though. Call me Tony. When two people have shared a kiss, lackluster though it was, not to mention a few spats, it's time to dispense with the formalities, don't you agree?"

Lisa forced herself to remain calm, despite his reference to the infamous kiss, which she knew he'd brought up deliberately to inflame her. "As you wish," she said mildly.

His eyes glittered and she saw that she hadn't deceived him. Even so, she had the impression he was a little disappointed that his goading hadn't brought about a fresh round of open fireworks.

The telephone was in the living room and though the television was still on, Lisa was acutely aware that her host was listening to her every word while she talked to Roni. After she explained the situation, her roommate was full of eager questions. "What's he like? Did you get the interview or was he furious?"

"I . . . we'll discuss it when I get home," she said, fielding the questions.

"Oh, I get it. He's right there in the room, is that it?" Roni asked.

"Yes. How's the cold?"

"Still here," Roni answered. "I was taking a nap this afternoon, and the doorbell rang, waking me up. Guess who it was."

"This is long distance, Roni," Lisa said wearily. "Besides, I'm not in the mood for guessing games. Tell me."

"Kevin. He was really disappointed that you weren't here. He said he'd call back tonight. What do you want me to tell him if he does?"

Lisa wasn't sure whether she was pleased with that bit of news or not. Two months ago he had walked out of her life, and on the whole she didn't think she wanted him back in it. It was just as well that she hadn't been there today.

"Just say you don't know when I'll be back."

"Okay," Roni said agreeably. "But when will you, really? Be home, I mean?"

"I don't know. It depends on getting the car fixed."

"Do you have enough money for it?" Roni asked anxiously.

"I have no idea," Lisa said. "I sure hope so. I'd better hang up now, Roni. Bye."

When she hung up the phone, she turned around to see that Tony Neugent was openly watching her . . . and had just as obviously been listening to every word she said.

Now, he got out of his chair and crossed the room. "So how's Ronnie taking the news that you're spending the night here in my cabin?" he asked with an edge of sarcasm to his voice.

Lisa shrugged. "Okay. Why?"

"You mean he's not jealous?"

She was puzzled for a moment, and then she realized he thought her roommate was a man. "Roni understands the situation," she said carefully.

"Does he?" He stepped closer. "You must have a very open relationship." He reached out and placed his hand beneath her chin, tipping her head back so that she had no choice but to look up into his eyes. "Doesn't Ronnie realize that we're a man and a woman, all alone together in a remote cabin without any chaperones? Doesn't he realize that anything, *anything*, might happen during the long night ahead?"

His voice was soft, suggestive and compelling. As had happened the previous night when she had been in his arms dancing, a languor stole over Lisa for a moment, rendering her oblivious of everything except his virile attractiveness and the animal magnetism that pulled at her senses.

As one strong arm slid around her waist, drawing her toward him, her right mind abruptly reasserted itself. She wrenched free of him, moved like lightning toward the fireplace and snatched up the poker.

"Nothing, nothing is going to happen here tonight!" she said decisively. "If you know what's good for you, you'll keep your distance!"

In two strides Tony was before her and quite calmly removing the poker from her tight grasp as easily as he might have brushed away a fly. "You're not going to hit anybody with that thing," he said as he replaced it where it belonged. "And I'm not going to bother you with any unwelcome attentions. I thought I'd already made that clear." He grinned. "I merely wondered what your lover thinks about your staying for the night. And how faithful you are to him."

"Roni," she said in as positive a voice as she could, "trusts me completely."

"Really? As beautiful as you are and given the uniqueness of our situation, your Ronnie must be a fool." He shook his head. "Actually, I've had quite enough of your company for one day. Entertaining reporters, even ones as sexy as you, isn't my style. I'm going to take a shower and hit the hay. You can watch television or read or do whatever you please. The spare bedroom's yours when you get ready to go to bed yourself."

He went down the hall and left Lisa standing there. Instead of having to defend her virtue, she was left to herself and her confused, chaotic thoughts.

Chapter Four

$\mathcal{I}$n eloquent apology for its tempestuous behavior the day before, the morning burst forth dazzlingly beautiful. Lisa awoke to the brilliance of sunlight flooding the unfamiliar room, and when she went to the window she saw a cloudless sky, a bird in flight and grassland, heavily coated with clinging moisture, glistening like millions of diamonds.

There was no sound within the house as she donned the oversized brown robe, opened the bedroom door and headed toward the bathroom. There she washed up and combed her hair and yearned for her toothbrush. Instead, she had to settle for rubbing some of Anthony Neugent's toothpaste across her teeth with a fingertip and helping herself to his mouthwash for good measure.

Tony's own bedroom door was open when she passed

it, revealing that its occupant was not there. Nor was he in the living room or kitchen. There was, however, the enticing scent of fresh coffee and again Lisa helped herself. She was already in debt to the man for a night's lodging and dinner, so she reasoned that these other small liberties could make little difference.

She had supposed he was tending to his cattle or horses, but when she carried her coffee out to the front porch, she saw a truck, which she correctly surmised was his, down near the entrance gate. Her car's front end was raised, and Tony's legs were the only part of him visible as they stretched out from beneath it.

Beyond the gate, Lisa could see that today the road was passable and the sight of it lifted her spirits. Small puddles of rainwater covered patches of the road as well as the long driveway, but there was no question about vehicles being able to get through.

She glanced dubiously at the muddy ground and then at her bare feet, peeking out from beneath the folds of the overlarge robe, and decided against walking down to join Tony. Instead, she went back inside to dress and start breakfast. The least she owed the man for trying to see about her car was a hot meal.

As soon as breakfast was ready, she called him. When he came, he was caked with mud. For one long electric moment their eyes locked and Lisa was a little dazed at the impact his presence made on her. Covered as he was by the mud, there was still a strong, virile and compelling aura emanating from him, tugging at her senses, throwing her into a state of confusion. Her mouth went dry and she could only look at him, at those dark eyes and the perfectly chiseled lips, while her heart began to skip erratically.

"Keep the food warm for me while I grab a quick shower, will you?" he asked at last. "I'm too filthy to sit down at the table like this."

Lisa nodded, unable to speak, and while he went toward the bathroom, she placed the stack of pancakes and sausages into the oven. Only then did she realize she hadn't asked about her car.

Fifteen minutes later, Tony rejoined her, looking wonderfully fresh and vigorous with damp hair and a healthy glow to his face. He wore snug-fitting jeans, tooled leather boots and a pale-yellow western shirt with the sleeves rolled up to the elbows. His powerful body seemed to dominate the room, dwarfing everything somehow, and again Lisa felt a strange, inexplicable breathlessness when he smiled at her as she set the food on the table.

"Looks good," he said approvingly. "Smells even better!"

Lisa spoke a little sharply in an effort to conceal the effect he was having on her. "Better try it before handing out any bouquets." She sat down and asked the question uppermost in her mind. "The car?"

Tony's smile faded as he poured syrup over his pancakes. "I'm a fair mechanic, Lisa. My hobby is tinkering with old cars, but the universal joint went out and no Band-Aid approach is going to work. I suspected that was the problem yesterday when it tipped over like it did. The drive shaft had fallen to the ground. I just didn't want to say anything until I could check it out. I'm really sorry."

Lisa shrugged, hoping her absolute despair wasn't

evident. Struggling to keep her voice steady, she said, "There's no need for you to be sorry. It's not your fault. Besides, you tried to help. So . . . what do you suggest I do?"

"We'll have to call a garage and have it towed," Tony told her. "I know a good garage in Santa Barbara."

Lisa swallowed hard and asked with dread, "How . . . how much do you estimate it'll cost?"

He told her and instantly she lost her appetite. She went pale and gazed at her plate, wondering how she would ever be able to afford it. Right now she didn't have that kind of money and neither did Roni. Until she got that check for the Mermaid Shampoo commercial she was living on a shoestring-thin budget that did not allow for major extras. She could, she supposed, call her father in Arizona and ask him for a loan, but she hated to do that. She was twenty-five years old and she'd been on her own for a long time now. The last thing she wanted was to be subsidized by her parents like a child, and even more important, she knew their finances were tight, too. Three years ago her father had taken a medical retirement. They had enough problems without taking on hers as well.

"You didn't hear a word I just said," Tony stated, interrupting her whirling thoughts. "What's the matter?"

"I . . ." Lisa's throat tightened and she found it difficult to speak. "I . . . don't have the money," she finally admitted.

Tony stared at her. "What did you say?"

Overwrought, Lisa was suddenly angry with him. "You heard me," she snapped. "I don't have the money to get the car repaired."

His eyebrows fell heavily over his eyes as he squinted at her, frowning. "Are you saying," he asked in a dangerously quiet voice, "that you expect *me* to foot the bill for you?"

Lisa's expression became incredulous. Waves of excruciating embarrassment swept over her, hot, lava hot. "No!" The word exploded between them. She thrust her chair away from the table and got to her feet, giving him a scathing look. "I know you have a low opinion of me!" she breathed. "You have since the first minute we met, but give me a break! Why on earth would you think I'd expect you to pay my bills?"

Tony had the grace to flush. He dropped his fork to his plate and also got to his feet, but Lisa turned away from him, burying her face in her hands, fighting tears of despair, frustration and consuming anger.

Her hands were pried from her face and caught in two large ones. Lisa bent her head to avoid looking at him and struggled without success to free herself from his touch.

"I'm sorry." Tony's voice was unexpectedly gentle. "I shouldn't have said that."

"You shouldn't have even thought it!" she said, sniffing. "You've got some nerve, you know that?" Again she tried to release her hands from his, but he thwarted the effort by tightening his clasp.

She heard him laugh softly. "Old habits die hard."

"What do you mean?" For the first time she lifted her head to look at him.

"Nothing," he said enigmatically. "Obviously it didn't apply to you. Now come back and eat the excellent breakfast that you cooked. It's getting cold."

Lisa grimaced. "I don't feel like eating anymore. I don't know what I'm going to do."

"Tell you what," Tony said. "I'll lend you the money. How's that?" At the sudden squall darkening her eyes, he added hastily, "With proper interest and everything."

Lisa shook her head and her hair bounced vigorously. "I don't want a penny of your money!" she exclaimed. "I'll manage on my own somehow." She tugged again and this time freed her hands from the prison of his. Then she sucked in a deep shuddering breath and added, because she had no choice, "But it's going to take some time. Will you be kind enough to allow me to leave the car here for two or three weeks? Just until I get the money together?"

"Sure, if that's what you want," he answered agreeably. "But honestly, I don't mind lending . . ." He stopped as she shook her head again, then shrugged. "Suit yourself." An odd, speculative look came into his eyes. "You know, I don't think I've ever met such an independent woman before."

"Is that bad?"

He grinned at her. "The jury's still out. Now sit down and eat like I told you."

They both returned to the table in a better humor, but though Lisa forced herself to eat because Tony insisted, she was still too worried to be able to enjoy it.

"I will have to impose upon you for one more favor," Lisa ventured after a while. "After breakfast, will you drive me to Santa Barbara so I can catch a bus back home?"

"There's no point in it, if you don't mind sticking

around here a few more hours. I'll be going back myself late this afternoon. You can ride with me.''

"I'd appreciate that very much," she answered in a subdued voice. "I . . . I'm really sorry I messed up your entire weekend so badly."

His eyes twinkled. "Oh, there have been moments that weren't all bad."

She wasn't sure just what he was referring to, whether he meant he'd actually enjoyed their arguments, the times when he'd embarrassed her by his needling comments or suggestive actions, not to mention the insult of that kiss, or the few times when they had actually gotten along like civilized people. She had a feeling it was wiser not to inquire.

Tony poured more coffee when they had finished the meal and asked, "Do you ride?"

Lisa nodded. "Sometimes, whenever I have the chance."

"I've got a few chores to do around here that'll keep me busy most of the morning and the man who manages things for me will be coming over to talk to me, so if you'd like to use one of the horses and go for a ride, you're quite welcome."

"Thanks, anyway," Lisa said ruefully, glancing down at her wrinkled skirt and blouse, "but this outfit is in bad-enough condition already. I'm afraid horseback riding would finish it off."

"I hadn't thought of that," he admitted. His gaze flickered over her objectively. "Maybe we can fix you up with something."

Lisa laughed outright and some of the tension she'd

been feeling drained away. She shook her head and said, "In case you hadn't noticed, there's a slight disparity in our clothes sizes. There's no way I could get by in anything of yours. Even if I could wear them, I don't have any shoes except my high heels."

Tony laughed, too. It was a hearty, pleasant sound that appealed to Lisa and made her think fleetingly that all men should have a laugh like his . . . open and uninhibited, a frank enjoyment of life.

"Hmmm, you have a point," he said after a moment. "You're so slender and delicate I could probably carry you with one arm and run the way I once did with a football." His gaze slowly traveled from her face downward, lingering on its journey so that Lisa caught her breath. His eyes were no longer impersonal and she was both alarmed and intrigued. Much to her disgust, she found herself wondering what it would be like to be kissed by him, really kissed, not like that deliberate attempt to anger her last night.

As his gaze returned to her face, there was a knowing look in his eyes and amusement lurked on his lips. It was as though he had read her mind and knew her ambivalent thoughts.

Lisa's face warmed. Abruptly, to avoid that devilish gaze, she got to her feet and began gathering up the dishes. "Go ahead and get started on your chores," she told him matter-of-factly as she turned her back to him. "I'll clean the kitchen."

To her relief, he left the room. Lisa busied herself washing the dishes, scrubbing as though her life depended on it. She would be very glad, she told herself, when she was away from this disturbing man once and for all. He had a way of keeping her off-balance, unsure of herself or of him and frankly, it was exhausting.

The subject of her thoughts suddenly returned. With a triumphant grin, Tony held up for her inspection a pair of jeans, a shirt and some brown leather shoes. *"Voilà!* I think these will do for you."

Lisa was startled. They were women's clothes. Some girlfriend of Tony's must have left them here. That lady, she was certain, wouldn't take kindly to another woman wearing them and Lisa shrank from the idea of even touching them.

Tony didn't seem to notice her reaction. He draped the pants and shirt over the back of a chair. "Maggie was here a couple of months ago and I suddenly remembered her saying she was leaving a few things she'd be using next time she came. They look like they're about your size. They might be a little bit large for you, but you can manage with them for one day."

"Who is Maggie?" Lisa carefully kept her tone casual. "Is she your girlfriend?"

Tony looked at her consideringly for a moment and then he grinned and nodded. "Yeah, she's my girl. My very best girl."

Lisa looked down at the plate she was washing and swallowed hard, ridiculously disappointed. Well, she had asked and she had found out and she had no business caring one way or another! But it was a moment before she could bring herself to face Tony again.

"I can't wear her clothes," she said in a dull voice.

"For Pete's sake, why not?" he asked, genuinely astonished.

"Be . . . just because. She wouldn't like it at all, I'm sure."

"Don't be silly. She wouldn't mind. Not my Maggie. She's a generous lady. Now don't argue about it anymore. As soon as you've changed, come out to the barn and I'll have Golden Boy saddled and ready for you."

He didn't give Lisa a chance to object again. With purposeful strides, he went through the living room and out the door, leaving her alone to get on with her washing and brooding.

Lisa allowed Golden Boy to amble where he would since Tony had assured her that even if she got lost, the horse would know his way back. It felt good to be outdoors beneath the bright sun, and the day was unexpectedly warm.

She passed a field of waving alfalfa and in another hillside pasture in the distance she could see the dark forms of cattle grazing. In the opposite direction loomed the Santa Ynez Mountains. In spite of the borrowed clothes, Lisa was enjoying herself and she could easily understand Tony's love for this place. Although it was only about twenty miles from the busy, urban area of Santa Barbara, there was a feeling of such complete peace and isolation about it that the hustle and bustle of civilization seemed a remote, bad dream.

She sucked in a sharp, deep breath of air and there was only the faintest tang of salty moisture from the ocean just scant miles away. The mountains and the forests of the nearby Los Padres National Park dominated here, lending a pleasant feeling of cool freshness.

What a crazy, chaotic weekend this had turned out to be! First the flat tire Friday night when she'd been dressed so absurdly and Tony had come along and helped her. Then, amazingly, Tony had turned out to be the man she'd wanted to interview! After that had come in quick succession his swift anger, the terror of her car going wild, the sudden fierce storm and the uneasy night staying alone with him in his cabin. Today there was the bad news about her car and now this, a pleasant horseback ride, just as though she were on vacation and had nothing at all to worry about!

But pleasant as this moment was, it was merely an illusion. She had plenty to worry about. It was bad enough that she was going to have to do without her car for a while, which wasn't going to be easy, but even more difficult was going to be the matter of paying for the repairs. She would, of course, use the check from the Mermaid Shampoo commercial to do it, but out of that check had to come payments for several other bills, too, including a rather large dental bill; and if she didn't soon get the money owed her from three articles that had recently been accepted by various publications, Lisa didn't know how she would even be able to buy groceries, much less keep up her half of the rent.

She sighed heavily, despair washing over her anew because of Tony's refusal to let her interview him. That meant kissing good-bye the permanent job with *Today's Journal* and it was a bitter disappointment. It also meant that she had no choice but to search for some other kind of work between now and Roni's wedding if she wanted to keep a roof over her head. The alternative of finding another roommate who would be as compatible as Roni was unthinkable. There *was* no one else like Roni and Lisa knew herself well enough to realize she would be utterly miserable sharing close living quarters with some woman she'd barely met.

She wondered if she dared broach the subject of the interview again with Tony. But then she shuddered as she recalled his abrupt rage when he'd realized who and what she was. Somewhere, sometime, he'd had a bad experience with a reporter that had made him lump the rest of them in the same refuse pile. Now, as Golden Boy carried her up a gentle rise, she wondered what had happened to make him feel that way. Professional athletes always received a lot of press and it seemed to Lisa that they benefited greatly from it. Look how many of them did commercials. Moreover, she was dead certain they drew far more money from such work, based on their public recognition, than someone like herself ever would! Still, the fact remained that Tony hated the press, and no matter how badly she needed his story, she wasn't likely to get it. No, after his outburst, she didn't have the courage to broach the subject again.

She felt a strange pang of dejection, knowing that after today it wasn't likely she would ever see him again. Tony Neugent intrigued her in a way no other man ever had, personally as well as professionally. He was undeniably good-looking and that was a part of it, but she had known other good-looking men who had left her cold. Yet something about him appealed to her and in the short time she had known him, she had already seen him in a number of moods from anger to teasing amusement to blatant sexuality.

Lisa was uncomfortable with that last thought and deliberately thrust it away. Golden Boy had topped the rise and down below, to her delight, was a narrow stream that wound through a small valley.

When she reached it, Lisa dismounted and, not trusting Golden Boy to abstain from deserting her, tied the reins to the branch of a nearby clump of chaparral before going down the slope toward the water.

For a long while, she sat on the bank beneath the shade of a birch tree, hands clasped around her legs, her chin propped on her knees as she gazed idly at the slow-moving water. At first her thoughts whirled around her precarious financial situation, but gradually she felt herself relaxing beneath the hypnotic spell of the water.

The day had warmed considerably, a striking contrast to the day before. As the sun moved in the sky, the shade of the tree moved with it and soon the heat grew uncomfortable. More and more the stream enticed Lisa. She hadn't gone swimming in a secluded spot like this since childhood and now she wondered if she dared.

But then, she decided impulsively, why not? Tony was occupied back at the barn and, from all indications, would remain so for hours yet. This was private property and there was no one to see her. She was as safe here from prying eyes as she would be in her own bathtub, so it would be a silly waste to deny herself such a simple pleasure.

Quickly, before the more conservative side of her nature could reason her out of it, Lisa stripped off her clothes and draped them on a low-hanging branch of the tree. She placed the shoes neatly next to the trunk, then turned and made her way down the bank toward the water, already delighting in the sensation of the warm sunshine on her bare skin.

The water was much colder than she'd expected and when she waded in, Lisa gasped as the frigid temperature jolted her nervous system. There was only one way, she knew from experience, to adjust to the difference in temperature in a hurry and that was to endure another moment of shocking unpleasantness by plunging herself entirely beneath the chilling water. She held her breath against the dreaded assault, then sank like a rock until the water swirled over her head.

When she came back to the surface, she took several deep breaths, brushed clinging wet tendrils of hair away from her face, and then partially submerged herself once more. The shock was already fading and now the water felt cool and refreshing as it closed about her, caressing her skin while the sun above kissed her face.

The stream was not very deep, she discovered. She could not actually swim in it, but she could, and did, float. Lying atop the water with the cool liquid buoying her and the sunshine heating her nude body was a blissful sensation that Lisa savored fully, knowing such a treat might never come her way again. With eyes closed, she thought of nothing, simply enjoying the exquisite combination of sun, water and the peacefulness of absolute solitude.

She wasn't even aware of the passage of time until she

heard Golden Boy whinny. The sound brought her back to reality. Though she was reluctant to end her stolen moments of pleasure, Lisa knew she should get dressed and head back toward the cabin. If she was gone too long, Tony might get concerned.

She allowed her legs to sink beneath the water until her feet touched bottom. Only then did she open her eyes and turn toward the bank.

Horror and excruciating embarrassment swept over her. Beneath the tree where she'd draped her clothes lounged Tony Neugent. He leaned against the trunk, legs stretched out before him, looking perfectly relaxed, as though he'd been there all day.

With an automatic reflex action, Lisa sank beneath the water until she was covered to her shoulders. Outrage shot through her, heating her despite the cool water that covered her. "You lousy Peeping Tom!" she sputtered. "How long have you been here?"

A mischievous grin spread across Tony's face. "Long enough to enjoy the scenery."

"If you had any decency at all, you'd have gone away again as soon as you saw me!"

"You've got to be kidding," he retorted. "No red-blooded man in his right mind would turn his back on such a delightful, titillating sight. It isn't every day that a fabled mermaid comes onto a man's own property and frolics in his stream. It's a fantasy come true." He sighed loudly and dramatically, then crossed his arms behind his head.

Lisa was so incensed she would have thrown something at him if she'd had anything to throw. She ached to wipe that smug expression off his face. As it was, however, she was hampered from doing anything except muttering unladylike words beneath her breath while she concentrated on keeping as much of her body as possible concealed underwater.

"All right," she said at last when she felt she had sufficient command of her emotions to speak again. "You've had your fun, but the joke's over. Now will you please leave so I can get dressed?"

"I'm not stopping you," he said mildly. "You can get dressed anytime you want."

The rage returned. "Damn you," she screamed, "go away! You know I'm not going to come out until you leave!"

"And I," came the reply, "have no intention of leaving. I've finished my work and I've got the rest of the day to relax and this is as good a spot as any to do it." He threw her a taunting look. "I've got an idea! Why don't I join you in the water?" He moved as though he were about to get up.

"Don't you dare!" Lisa hissed in panic. "I swear if you come in, I'll drown you!"

"Tsh! Tsh! Such a temper," Tony said mildly. He leaned back against the tree again. "All right, I'd just as soon stay here while you finish your swim. I'm in no hurry to get back to the city if you're not." He tipped his hat down so that it half covered his face.

Aggravated beyond measure, Lisa stared at him with stormy eyes, although with his hat lowered, he seemed entirely oblivious of her fury. "Will you *please* go away?" she begged after a few moments when he didn't move.

"Leave me alone," he muttered. "I'm taking a *siesta*."

"Go do it someplace else!" Lisa's voice was shrill and desperate.

To her annoyance, he didn't reply, nor did he respond to the next few comments she made, but finally when she called him a colorful and not very polite name, he lifted the hat and fixed his stern gaze on her. "Is that any way to speak to a man you want to interview?"

Lisa glared at him. "It's how I'd speak to any scoundrel. Now stop this little game of yours and go away. I'm getting cold!" She shivered and rubbed her arms. The action drew her further out of the water than she had intended and when she saw his gaze slip downward to the mound of her breasts, she hastily lowered herself again.

Tony chuckled. "I told you, you can come out anytime you like."

He lowered the hat over his face once more, settled himself comfortably against the tree and closed his eyes. He was enjoying himself hugely. It felt good to knock a cocky reporter down a peg or two and besides, she'd brought the whole thing on herself. When he'd set out to find Lisa, he'd expected to join her for an entirely casual ride over his land. When instead he'd spotted Golden Boy tied up near the stream and had seen her clothes flapping from a tree branch, he could no more have forgone the temptation to tease her than he could have stopped breathing.

All the same, though he had refused to leave just to annoy her, he'd decided it was best if he ceased looking at her. Lisa Knight was one hell of a beauty when she was wearing clothes, whether they were sexy outfits like that mermaid costume she'd worn the other night, an enormously oversized man's robe or a neatly tailored skirt and blouse, but seeing her floating on the water without a stitch on had practically knocked the breath out of him. Her cream-colored skin; her long, shapely legs; her smooth, curved hips; and her full breasts proudly protruding from the water had utterly dazzled him. Even if he'd wanted, he would've been unable to look away. He'd been completely mesmerized by such wondrous perfection.

Now, though, while she was hiding her charms beneath the water, it was best to get himself in hand. He reminded himself again that Lisa was a representative of the hated press. No matter how tempting or alluring she seemed, in truth she was the enemy and he couldn't afford to forget that just because she stirred up his natural physical instincts. There were other women just as beautiful and less dangerous. Forget her, forget her, forget her, he repeated silently while he gritted his teeth.

Things were quiet for so long from the direction of the stream that Tony began to feel slightly concerned. She wouldn't have gone downstream, would she? There would be no point to it since her clothes were here. Maybe she was in trouble, although that, too, seemed incredible. Lisa had appeared perfectly at home in the water, and besides, he knew it wasn't very deep. Still, the silence . . .

He was just about to make a move to tip back his straw hat so that he could see when he heard first water sloshing and then grass rustling. She was coming out at last.

Tony relaxed, carefully keeping still and, with difficulty, restraining a smile as he listened to her stealthy approach up the bank.

He felt her presence as she came near. His entire body became alert and tense. His nerve ends tingled and instantaneous desire shot a red-hot message throughout his body.

Forgetting his resolve of only moments ago about the inadvisability of becoming involved with a woman like Lisa, Tony tipped back his hat and opened his eyes. With her bare backside to him, Lisa was stepping into her panties. The exquisiteness of her body assaulted him anew and his mouth went dry.

As Lisa reached for her bra, she had to half turn toward him. When she did, she saw him watching her. Instantly, color surged to her face and she quickly turned away. "I thought you were asleep," she said bitterly. "You tricked me!"

In one swift movement, Tony tossed aside his hat, swung to his feet and without giving it a second thought, it seemed so natural and right, his arms went around Lisa. He pulled her against him so that her bare, moist back was pressed to his chest and he bent his head to press a kiss to one gleaming shoulder. She smelled of water and, it seemed to him, of sunshine and fresh air.

"I didn't intend to trick you," he murmured huskily. "Honestly, I didn't intend to look at you at all. I was only teasing you before. But I could feel you near me and I just couldn't stop myself. You're gorgeous, you know . . . the most beautiful woman I've ever seen." His hands tightened around her waist as he buried his face in her hair, and then, finding her neck, he began dropping kisses to the sensitive skin.

Lisa was stunned. Where had the hatred gone? The taunts? He sounded so different from before, even a little breathless. She was having trouble just then with her own breath. She was aware of a warm, magnetic response within herself; she was also aware that there was a danger in that response, although at that moment, the reason behind it escaped her.

She gave a slight shake to her head, as though to clear it. "I . . . I think you'd better let me go," she said softly, without conviction. As she spoke, Tony's head bent lower and his lips gazed the ridge of her collarbone. Without being aware that she was doing it, Lisa tipped her head back and toward the side, allowing him better access, and as his hands began to slide up her rib cage, strange little tremors shook her.

"I can't let you go," Tony whispered. His breath was warm and silky against her neck, shooting little tingles through her. "I simply can't."

His lips moved back to her shoulder and at the same time his hands moved upward to cup her breasts. A sudden liquid fire unlike any Lisa had ever known ignited within her. She closed her eyes and allowed the fire to lick through her veins unchecked.

After a time, Tony gently turned her in his arms, lifted her face and bent to kiss her. Lisa's lips parted to accept it willingly, as urgent desires clamored through her body. Time and place lost relevance. The gurgling sound of the stream receded; they were unaware of the breeze stirring about them or of the hum of insects; neither the sunlight nor the dappling shade of the tree reached their consciousness; there were only the powerful emotions that consumed them . . . and each other.

Lisa drifted on a cloud as exquisite sensations raced through her, one right after the other. It was as though her body had been created just for this, for this man and his hands that brought such surges of great pleasure to her. Yet pleasurable though it was, there was an incompleteness to it and a feeling of urgency to bring such sensations to a conclusion.

At the same time, she wanted the feelings never to end. As Tony's hands moved slowly and caressingly over her, Lisa was enthralled. Never had she felt more womanly, more vital, more alive! The pressure of his strong, masculine body close to hers made her heart pound with excitement. Her own hands roamed over his arms, his shoulders and his chest, and she loved every inch of the exploration. With a boldness hitherto unrealized, she tugged his shirt free of his jeans and unbuttoned it so that she could continue the exploration unfettered.

Abruptly, Tony crushed her to him, pressing her sensitive breasts to the hard wall of his chest, and when he kissed her this time it was so intense, so filled with desperate hunger, that it was almost punishing to them both.

At last Tony groaned against her lips. "I want you so badly, I'm half-crazy."

Bending, he put one arm around her shoulders and one at her knees and lowered her to the soft carpet of grass. Then, with dark passion glittering in his eyes as he gazed at her, he reached for his belt buckle.

But in that one instant, timelessness faded for Lisa, and with excruciating pain, she returned to her senses. Quickly, she sat upright and held out a restraining hand.

"N-no!" Her voice quavered as she got to her feet. "No, Tony. This is all wrong. I . . . can't go through with it!"

His hands froze at his waistband. "What did you say?" The words came out slowly, measured . . . and with unmistakable shock.

Lisa darted past him and, with a trembling hand, picked up her bra and covered her exposed breasts. "I said I can't. It . . . it's wrong. We don't even know one another. We're strangers!" She turned her back to Tony while she hooked the bra.

With a hint of thinly concealed violence, Tony was suddenly beside her. He grabbed her arm and whirled her around until they were face-to-face. His eyes were almost completely black, as black as the dark emotions that filled him.

"What kind of a woman are you, to lead a man on that way and then throw on the brakes? Does torture give you some sort of perverse pleasure or what?" His gaze narrowed and he glared at her with contempt before he turned his back to her, snatched up his abandoned shirt and hat and strode off toward the tethered horses.

A thick lump clogged Lisa's throat as she watched Tony swing into his saddle and ride away. Only when he was out of sight did she finish dressing and she did it with a heavy heart. What had she done? she asked herself miserably. If what she'd done was right, then why did she feel so awful?

When she reached the barn a half hour later, Tony materialized from its interior. Wordlessly, he began to remove the saddle and bridle from Golden Boy as soon as she'd dismounted. Lisa couldn't bear the cold silence and, fighting back tears, said to his stiff, broad back, "Tony, I'm . . . really sorry. I . . . neither of us should have gotten so carried away, that's all. But honestly, I . . . I'm not a tease."

"You could have fooled me," he said in a harsh voice. He jerked his head around to look at her. "Do you have a husband you somehow forgot to mention?"

"No." Lisa looked down at the churned earth beneath her feet. It was too painful to see the anger and accusation in his eyes.

"A fiancé, then?"

"No."

"Ah, but there's Ronnie, isn't there? Your live-in boyfriend. I'd forgotten him."

"No!" Lisa's spirit reasserted itself. "The one you forgot was Maggie!"

"Maggie?" Tony stared at her and seemed genuinely mystified.

"Your girlfriend!" Lisa reminded him impatiently.

"Oh. Yes. I suppose I did forget. Not that it would be of interest to her one way or another. Well, no matter," he went on, shrugging his shoulders. "Your self-control saved the day and you can go home to your lover with a clear conscience."

"You have no conscience at all," Lisa exclaimed, "if you think cheating on your girlfriend wouldn't matter to her. What kind of a man are you?"

"A more honest man than you are a woman, because I play fair. Maggie, for all I adore her more than any woman on earth, isn't a girlfriend in the sense you mean. She's more like family. So, you see, I wasn't being disloyal to anyone. If there's anything I detest more than a reporter, it's a dishonest woman and I've had a little experience in that department, so I can spot one a mile away. You," he ended brusquely, "happen to be both."

"When did I lie to you?" Lisa demanded.

"When you refused to finish what you started," he said bluntly.

Lisa flinched beneath the assault of his scalding words. The truth of them was undeniable.

"I've apologized for that," she said quietly, "and I wish you would accept it. But I just couldn't go through with . . . well, you know. Tony, we hardly even know each other. I can't make . . . make love with a man who's a stranger!"

A sneer crossed Tony's face. "I wondered when we'd get back to the subject of the interview. What're you trying to do, drive a bargain?" He shook his head. "Forget it! I've never had to submit to an inquisition with a woman before and I'm not about to start now. No matter how alluring your charms are," he added scornfully as his eyes raked her body.

"You're disgusting!" Lisa snapped. "I may want an interview, but not badly enough to sell myself! You're being crass and deliberately misinterpreting what I said."

"Maybe," he surprised her by agreeing. "But perhaps it's better for us both that way. Why don't you go get changed into your own clothes,'' he added wearily. ''As soon as I'm done here, we'll head for home.''

Frustrated and not knowing what else to do, Lisa did as he'd suggested. Inside the privacy of the bedroom she'd used, she struggled to regain some semblance of calm. After all, there was still the long drive ahead during which she and Tony would be forced to endure one another's company. It would be easier if they put on a façade of indifferent politeness. Otherwise, the whole thing was going to be intolerable.

When she entered the living room, Tony was just answering the telephone. Lisa couldn't avoid overhearing him speak.

''Hello? Oh, hi, Maggie, my love! How are you?'' His voice was warm and filled with unmistakable, genuine affection.

Just like a member of the family, hmmm? Lisa thought furiously as she went outside to wait on the porch. Tony Neugent had a hell of a nerve calling her dishonest when it was apparent even to an idiot that he'd been lying through his teeth!

But what angered her most of all was the sharp stab of jealousy she felt toward the unseen Maggie.

Chapter Five

It was four-thirty in the afternoon by the time they reached the fringes of Malibu. Not a single word had been spoken between them since leaving the ranch. The heavy silence was so thick it would have taken a machete to chop through it and Lisa was also suffering from a headache brought on by the unbearable tension.

"Where do you live?"

The sound of Tony's voice jolted her. Lisa withdrew her gaze from the ocean waves and glanced toward him. His broad shoulders looked as rigid and inflexible as the green hillsides that held themselves so proudly above the sea. His profile, too, was unyielding, strong and set as it must once have looked when he was about to do battle on a football field.

Although he must have been aware that she had turned

to look at him, Tony kept his own gaze on the road. There was nothing in his demeanor or his question to indicate any softening of his anger toward her. Lisa swallowed over the burning ache in her throat and it was a moment before she felt in sufficient control of her voice to answer.

"Santa Monica. Is that out of your way?"

Tony shrugged. "It doesn't matter," came the flat, colorless reply.

"Where do you live?" she asked. Los Angeles, with its many different communities, was a sprawling monster, and for the first time it occurred to Lisa that it might be extremely inconvenient for him to drive her all the way home.

"Here," Tony said.

"Here? You live here in Malibu?"

He nodded. "See that white roof?" He pointed toward the endless row of expensive beachfront homes. "About three houses down?"

Lisa looked and nodded. "Is that your house?"

"Yes." Tony drove past it.

Lisa turned toward him again, chagrined. "Then, please, just drop me at a restaurant or somewhere like that," she begged. "I'll call my roommate to come get me. There's no need for you to put yourself out by driving me all the way home."

"I'll see you home," Tony said firmly.

"But really," Lisa protested urgently, "I can't keep putting you out! If you'll just drop me—"

"I said I'd drive you home," Tony interrupted in a voice as hard as steel.

Unhappily, Lisa fell silent again and they both remained

that way until they reached Santa Monica and were skirting Palisades Park. Only then did she speak and it was to give him directions.

A few minutes later the Porsche slid to a halt in the parking area of the apartment complex where Lisa lived. Forcing herself to be polite, she turned to Tony and said stiffly, "I want to thank you for all your hospitality. And for giving me a lift home. I . . ." Here she hesitated, feeling like a fool; yet her upbringing dictated that she at least put forth the effort. "Would you like to come in for a cup of coffee? I know you must be tired."

For the first time all afternoon, he looked directly at her and there was surprise in his eyes. There was also a dry irony in his voice. "Thanks," he said coldly, "but I have a feeling your boyfriend wouldn't appreciate it very much."

Lisa gazed at him thoughtfully. "You know, you make an awful lot of snap judgments. You made up your mind right from the beginning that I was a terrible person because I happen to write for a living. This afternoon you put a few ugly interpretations on what happened instead of giving me the right to say I'd made a mistake and wanted to back out, and you also leapt to your own wrong conclusion about my roommate. Roni," she added as she jumped out of the car, "is a girl." She slammed the door and strode toward the sidewalk.

Almost instantly, Tony was striding beside her. "I've changed my mind about the coffee," he said conversationally. "I'd like some after all."

"The offer's no longer open," Lisa said resentfully. She walked faster.

"In that case, let me take you someplace for a drink."

Lisa stopped dead in her tracks. "Look, I only offered to be polite. You know good and well you don't want to be with me any more than I want to be with you. You haven't spoken a word to me all afternoon, civil or otherwise, and frankly, I'm tired of all the tension. Who needs it?"

Tony suddenly smiled and the transformation from the grim face he'd worn all afternoon was astonishing. He held out a hand toward her and said with engaging frankness, "Okay, I know I've behaved like a spoiled kid who didn't get his way, but you have to admit I really had a reason to pout. I'm sorry. Now, can we call a truce and can I have that coffee? I really could use it."

A tiny smile twitched the corners of Lisa's mouth in spite of her annoyance. Reluctantly she extended her hand. "All right. Truce."

Tony shook her hand and then dropped it with unflattering haste. "Lead the way," he said lightly.

They followed the sidewalk toward the cluster of modern brick-and-wooden buildings. The surroundings were pleasing with neat, green lawns, eucalyptus trees and colorful flower beds. Orange-and-yellow marigolds centered one large area, encircled by pink-and-white daisies. Edging the apartment buildings were beds of roses and geraniums.

Lisa led Tony up the stairs to a long balcony and there she paused before a door while she found her key.

When they entered the apartment, Roni, dressed in jeans and a T-shirt, was curled up in her favorite chair reading a novel. She looked up expectantly, but then surprise and something oddly akin to dismay flickered across her face as Tony followed Lisa into the room.

The young woman immediately got to her feet and Lisa introduced them.

"Roni, this is Anthony Neugent. Tony, my roommate, Veronica Wallace."

Tony offered his hand, and as the girl clasped his he felt it tremble slightly. It surprised him so much that it caused him to look at her more closely. There was something vaguely familiar about her. He'd seen that dark head before and that flashing, vivacious smile, but he couldn't seem to place just where. Certainly he didn't remember the nervousness.

"Have we met before?" he asked curiously as he released her hand.

"No. Never." Her eyes darted to Lisa and in a rush, as though she were anxious to change the subject, she asked, "Did you get your car fixed?"

Lisa shook her head and Tony was struck by the sudden, odd nervousness about her, too. Something was going on here and he was the only one who didn't know what it was. Both the girls were covering up and since the only question he'd asked was whether he'd met the girl named Roni before, he had a hunch he'd been right, only for some reason neither one of them wanted to admit it.

Tony stared fixedly at the girl he'd just met while Lisa explained what had happened to her car. He knew they had met before, or at least he'd seen her someplace. But had it been some social occasion or in a business setting? He tried to think of various business offices he'd visited recently, of the women he'd met working in them, and because he had an excellent memory, it suddenly hit him.

"You work at the Cameron Children's Foundation," he stated. "I remember seeing you there."

Both girls looked at him with anxious faces and Roni paled visibly.

"I . . . er, yes, I do. Although we were never introduced," she added hastily.

The connection was finally made in Tony's mind. He pressed his lips together and gazed thoughtfully at Roni. "Now I understand how Lisa found out about my supposedly secret donation."

Roni went even whiter and looked sick.

Lisa spoke quickly. "Please don't blame her, Tony. She told me about it, yes, the way roommates share things about their work. But she had no idea I'd try to get a story about it from you and in fact she begged me not to see you."

"Hmmm," Tony said noncommittally. He crossed his arms and his gaze moved slowly from one girl's face to the other.

"W-what are you going to do?" Roni asked at last. Her voice was thick with anxiety.

"What would you do if your confidentiality had been violated?"

Roni glanced down at the floor, unable to reply.

"You're not going to report her, are you?" Lisa asked.

Tony's eyes narrowed. "Shouldn't I?"

"She'll be fired if you do!" Lisa exclaimed. "Surely you can't be that cruel and heartless!"

Tony relented. "No," he said in a low voice. "I can't."

Roni looked up then and favored him with a dazzling smile. "Thank you! I'm really sorry and I promise it'll never happen again."

He grinned at her. "It'd better not. If you must tell secrets, maybe you'd better get a roommate who's not a journalist."

Roni giggled. "I'll do just that in a few more months. I'm getting married at Christmas."

Tony chuckled. "I take it he's not a snoopy reporter like some of us present in this room?"

Roni shook her head. "He's a police officer going to night school and working toward his law degree."

"A good choice. Perhaps he'll be able to police your tongue," Tony teased, "or, at the very least, be able to represent you in court if it ever comes to that."

"It won't be necessary," Roni said with an engaging smile. "I've learned my lesson. I'll never blab another secret!"

"Unless it's in your sleep," Lisa gibed. Apparently deciding it was time to drop the uncomfortable subject, even though it had worked out to her satisfaction, she turned to Tony and smiled. "I promised you coffee. Sit down and make yourself comfortable. I'll be back in a couple of minutes."

"I'll help you," Roni offered, following Lisa out of the room. "I'm afraid I've got bad news. The fridge went on the blink yesterday and I had to call in a repairman."

"Oh, no," Lisa groaned. "Did it set us back much?"

"I hate to even tell you," Roni replied.

Tony sat down in a white-cushioned easy chair. It was absurd, after having been so angry earlier, but he'd felt lighthearted ever since Lisa had admitted that her roommate was a female, not a man. Logic told him it shouldn't matter one way or another, but somehow logic was taking a backseat. For the moment he felt content.

Through the partially open kitchen door, he could hear the low-voiced conversation of the two girls. They were still discussing the cost of the refrigerator repair and then Lisa asked, "Did any of my magazine checks come in the mail yesterday?"

"Not a one," Roni replied.

Lisa sounded gloomy. "If some of my money doesn't start coming in from somewhere, I'm going to be flat broke by the end of the month."

"I know," Roni said worriedly. "After paying my car insurance this month, I'm short, too, and I'm not going to be able to cover your share of the rent. Let's just hope at least a couple of your checks get here before the first."

Tony listened thoughtfully as his gaze wandered around the room. While the apartment complex itself was fairly new and nice-looking, it was not luxurious. In fact, it was exactly the sort of place one would expect two single working girls to live. However, he was a little puzzled by the quiet, understated elegance around him. Soft white drapes gave the room a muted brightness. The sofa was upholstered in a delicate, creamy-aqua linen and the color was picked up by throw pillows in the chair where he was sitting and in a white-painted rocking chair opposite him. Tasteful flower prints on the wall were also framed by pale-aqua-colored matting. Scattered about the room were tropical plants, some in large pots on the floor, others in dainty baskets on tables, several hanging from the ceiling before the window. The entire atmosphere was of restful, spacious beauty and Tony was a little suspicious of the seeming anxiety about money he was hearing from the kitchen when he could tell at a glance that quite a bit of money had been spent furnishing this room alone.

The two girls returned with the tray of coffee and after pouring Tony's cup, Lisa excused herself. "If you don't mind," she said, "I'll leave Roni to entertain you for a few minutes while I change. I really can't tolerate this wrinkled skirt and blouse another minute."

While she was gone, Tony said idly, "You have a lovely apartment here . . . and beautiful things. Did you hire a decorator to do it for you?"

Roni's laughter was reminiscent to Tony of tinkling bells. "Would I be so concerned about keeping my job if we had that kind of money, Mr. Neugent?" she asked in genuine amusement.

Tony grinned. "Call me Tony. And I don't know. Would you?"

"Lisa did nearly all of the decorating herself, actually, and we got by on very little," Roni told him with a certain pride in her voice. "We bought the furniture at flea markets and refinished the wood pieces together. We got the fabrics at a wholesale outlet and Lisa reupholstered the sofa and chair and also made the draperies and pillows. She's even the one with the green thumb," she added ruefully. "She gets cuttings from friends' plants and then they grow wild. Sometimes it's a jungle in here!"

Tony was honestly amazed. "I had no idea she was so

talented. She could easily become a professional decorator."

"I know. Or a dress designer, for that matter. Ever since we were in college she's sewn most of our clothes and if I say so myself, when we get dressed up, we're second best to no one! I wouldn't have a fourth as many nice clothes as I do if I had to buy them ready-made. Which," she said with a grimace, "I suppose I'll have to get used to doing after I'm married. That's one thing I'm going to miss about having Lisa around."

The doorbell rang and Roni went to answer it. A pleasant-looking man in his late twenties came in, swept her into his arms and kissed her soundly. When she led him toward Tony and introduced him as her fiancé, Tony grinned as he got to his feet and said dryly, "I assumed as much by the enthusiastic greeting. I'm Tony Neugent."

The other man grinned and they shook hands. "Jack Tilton. If I'd known Roni had such a famous visitor, I might have tempered the enthusiasm a little."

"He isn't my visitor, silly. He's Lisa's. I was just telling him how much I'm going to miss all Lisa's domestic talents after I marry you."

"So am I," Jack said with a twinkle in his eyes. "You, my love," he continued, stooping to kiss her nose, "can't cook worth two cents. Maybe I'm marrying the wrong girl."

"What?" Roni exclaimed, nudging him with an elbow.

Lisa came in from the bedroom. She had changed into jeans and a loose-fitting shirt and her hair was brushed back behind her ears and tied with a ribbon. The scene in the room had drastically deteriorated from when she'd left a few minutes ago. Jack and Roni appeared to be wrestling while Tony stood to one side openly laughing at them.

"What's going on here?" she demanded.

Roni pretended to pout. "Jack's thinking about swapping me in and marrying you instead . . . all because he loves your fricasseed chicken!"

"I don't know if that's the only reason," Jack said dreamily. "Her beef Stroganoff's pretty tempting, too."

Lisa laughed. "Jack, you may like my cooking, but you wouldn't marry me on a bet. I would never stand on a busy street corner and serenade you!"

Jack grinned and hugged Roni to his side. He looked at Tony and explained, "On my birthday, we were walking down the sidewalk toward the restaurant where we were going to have dinner. This one stops all of a sudden and starts singing 'Happy Birthday' at the top of her lungs. Before I knew what was happening, I was surrounded by this whole crowd of strangers who were all singing while Roni's waving her arms in the air like she's directing the Metropolitan Orchestra!"

Tony chuckled with appreciation. "Well, you've got to admit it's not a birthday you're likely to forget. There can't be many women like her around."

"That's a fact!" Jack smiled fondly at the girl beside him. "I guess I'll have to marry her just to be able to hang around and see what she's going to do next."

"Tell Tony how the two of you met," Lisa said with a laugh.

Jack did as the four of them sat down. After a while, he brought up the subject of Tony's football career and they soon launched into a rehash of the last Super Bowl. Lisa made another pot of coffee and by the time she served it the conversation had become more general. Lisa was a little surprised to see how well the two men were getting along. It seemed a little odd that a millionaire would have so much in common with a police officer.

When there finally came a lull in the conversation, Jack happened to glance down at his watch. "At the risk of getting my beloved all upset again," he said to Lisa, "what do you say to making lasagna for our dinner if I go out and buy all the fixings?"

Roni made a face at him. "You and your stomach! Still, that does sound good," she added after consideration. "Are you tired, Lisa, or do you feel up to cooking tonight?"

Lisa shrugged. "I don't mind. I'm not tired at all."

Tony instantly got to his feet. "I'd better be running along. Thanks for the coffee, Lisa." He turned toward the other couple, adding, "It was nice meeting—"

"Don't run off!" Roni protested, cutting off his words. "Stay and have dinner with us."

Uncertainty crossed Tony's face and when his gaze returned to Lisa she saw the silent question in his eyes. Strangely, he seemed unsure of his welcome and, equally surprising, she found herself suddenly, fiercely, wanting him to stay.

She smiled and said so. "I'd really like it if you did."

"Sure?" His eyes grew dark and they both remembered the embarrassing and awful storm that had passed between them hours earlier.

Lisa's face colored delicately. All the same, she steadfastly continued to meet his gaze. "I'm sure."

Tony smiled, breaking the thread of tension between them. "All right, then. I'd love to." He turned to Jack and added, "How about letting me go along with you to pick up the groceries? I'll buy the wine."

"It's a deal." Jack got to his feet.

As soon as the two men were gone, Roni asked eagerly, "Did you get the interview?"

"Not no, but emphatically no," Lisa answered. She began gathering up the empty coffee cups.

"Really?" Roni looked disappointed. "He seems so friendly and after he was so nice to me about spilling his secret to you, I was sure he must have agreed."

"Well, he didn't. I'm no better off now than I was when I left here yesterday. If anything, I'm a lot worse. Now I've not only got to get my car fixed, but when I can't deliver the story, *Today's Journal* won't deliver me that job. And I want it so bad I can taste it!"

"I know. Tony really is a recluse when it comes to publicity, isn't he?" Roni mused. "I wonder why."

"I wonder why, too," Lisa said. "What's more, I intend to find out first thing tomorrow. I'm going to the library and look up everything I can about Mr. Anthony Neugent."

The evening turned out to be fun. Tony, who was no more afraid of the kitchen than Lisa, helped her prepare the meal, while Jack and Roni mostly got in the way.

Tony teased them about starving to death after the wedding and Jack somberly acknowledged the possibility.

"As soon as I'm practicing law and can afford it, we'll have to hire a cook."

"Until then we'll live on peanut butter sandwiches, TV dinners and love," Roni said, laughing.

"And hopefully an occasional meal from Lisa, if she's humane," Jack tossed in.

Over dinner under Tony's interested questions, Jack talked about his work and Roni mentioned various things the foundation did to help youngsters. "One of the things we sponsor is inner-city swimming and softball teams for kids who couldn't afford it otherwise. Jack's gotten a bunch of his fellow officers together and they all do volunteer work with the kids."

"You manage a team?" Tony asked with interest.

Jack nodded.

"That's terrific."

"Not as terrific as donating a million dollars to build them a summer camp."

Tony shrugged it off. "Why not? I wouldn't have given it if I hadn't had it to give. It's no more than what you and your friends are doing."

"Didn't I read somewhere that you go around visiting junior high and high school football teams, giving them pep talks?"

Tony grinned. "Yeah, but don't go getting the idea that's a kindness on my part. I really get a kick out of talking with them and tossing the ball a few times. Sometimes I really think I should have gone into coaching instead of the business world after I left the pros. When I see some of those kids giving it all they've got, I have a sense of *déjà vu*. I see myself when I was their age and I know how important it is to have a caring, encouraging coach. I would never have gotten where I did without the dedicated interest of my high school coach.''

Lisa listened thoughtfully. The few glimpses she had into Tony's personality revealed a complex man. He might hate the press with an illogical vehemence and, from some things he'd said about women and dishonesty, be rather cynical where they were concerned, but on the other hand he obviously had equally deep feelings about children and people who'd helped him along life's road. A man who gave away so much money on behalf of children, besides giving of his time to encourage youngsters in the sport he loved, had to have a lot of compassion. He also seemed to be the sort who didn't get so big or famous that he forgot to be grateful to those who'd given him a boost when he'd needed it. Once again she wished he would relent and give her the interview she'd asked for, but this time it was more out of genuine curiosity about the man and what made him tick than because she wanted the job it would have enabled her to get. There was a lot more to Tony Neugent than met the eye.

Two hours later when they said good-bye at her door, she hoped against all reason that he would suggest seeing her again, but he did not. Politely, he thanked her for the evening, and just as politely, she thanked him for putting her up overnight and driving her home. Somehow, suddenly, the old awkward tension between them had returned. Lisa hated it, but there didn't seem to be any words that could end it.

When she went to bed shortly afterward, she had trouble falling asleep. She kept remembering Tony's smile, the teasing glint in his eyes and, most of all, the way she had felt when he'd held her. Just thinking about it brought a warm flush to her entire body. She had come dangerously close to throwing away all caution, but fortunately good sense had returned to her just in the nick of time. If she had allowed him to make love to her, she would detest herself now. As far as Lisa was concerned, such a thing should be reserved only for two people who genuinely cared about each other, not indulged in simply because of physical attraction. All the same, her treacherous body was even now betraying her by a strong desire that her mind could not eradicate.

The next morning, after dropping Roni off at her office, Lisa borrowed her roommate's car for the remainder of the day.

She drove to the downtown central library of Los Angeles where she knew she'd have the best chance of finding all the information she was seeking.

The library was an imposing edifice set amid a beautiful landscape of laurel, cypress, olive, palm and acanthus trees. As she mounted the steps that led from one terraced level to the next, her eyes surveyed the buff-colored stucco building with its sculptures above the entrance and the still higher tower that was topped by a Spanish-tiled geometric pyramid and a sculptured hand that held a torch. It perfectly exemplified the theme "Light and Learning."

Inside, however, she did not spend time appreciating

the murals as she often did. She was intent upon her mission: to find out what she could about Anthony Neugent.

Two hours later she knew a whole lot more about him than she had before and, to a large degree, had come to understand his aversion to publicity as well. She also felt like something of a Peeping Tom.

When she went outside again, the sunlight seemed blinding to her tired eyes. She had scanned every sports magazine article she could find about him and had read more slowly the microfilmed local newspaper accounts of his palimony suit.

As she headed toward the car, still slightly dazed from what she had discovered, the faintest snatches of memory returned as Lisa vaguely recalled seeing some of the news about it at the time. But not knowing the participants and being busy with her own life at the university, she'd paid scant attention.

A young starlet named Carmen Woods, who'd had bit parts in several movies and to whom Tony admitted having been engaged a year and a half prior to the lawsuit, took him to court and claimed he was the father of her baby. Tony fought the case by bringing in witnesses who testified she had been with other men while engaged to him and that that, in fact, was the reason for the breakup of their engagement. Blood tests didn't help. Typing proved Tony's and the child's blood were the same kind and even Lisa had to admit to herself that the press rode Tony pretty hard. There were several photos of him entering or leaving the courthouse with a grim expression as members of the press snapped photos or shoved microphones in his face.

A surprise witness, an out-of-work actor, came forth in Tony's defense, revealing his long-time secret relationship with Carmen and offering papers to prove that the two of them had taken a three-month trip together to Europe during the time in which she had become pregnant. Tony was cleared and the case was dropped. All the same, Tony's name had been smirched while Carmen Woods had derived a lot of wonderfully sympathetic press and an accompanying boost to her career as a direct result of the publicity. Ever since, she'd made a substantial climb in the entertainment industry. Recently Lisa had read that she'd just signed a contract to star in her own TV series. It all explained a lot about Tony's bitter cynicism concerning the integrity of women, not to mention his belief that the press as a whole was biased and cruel.

Lisa had also found that Tony's relationship with reporters, or at least some of them, had been less than cordial ever since he had entered the pros. He even punched out one reporter who wrote for a sports magazine. That man threatened a lawsuit, but eventually it was dropped. She had read a story done by the man about Tony and while it revealed some things about his past that he might not have enjoyed seeing in print, the article had actually made her feel quite compassionate toward the child he had been. If what was written was true, Tony had been abandoned by his father as an infant, by his mother when he was ten and then had been shuffled through a series of foster homes until a high school football coach and his wife took him in to live with them at age fourteen. No wonder the adult Tony cared so much about underprivileged or abused children, she thought as tears sprang to her eyes.

An entire week passed during which Tony was extremely busy. With his company lawyers, he studied the feasibility of purchasing a plant that manufactured computer parts and, with top advisers, went over the plans of putting together a new package deal for investors in a land development project. He scheduled early and late meetings every day and filled his calendar during regular business hours. All the same, he frequently found time to think of Lisa.

At least a dozen times he had picked up the telephone to call her, only to hang up again before he made the connection. He told himself he was crazy for wanting to see her again. In fact, stark, raving mad! A woman like that couldn't be trusted. Hadn't she already proved that? Whenever he thought about that scene between them down by the stream he was filled with a complicated mixture of anger, disgust and frustrated yearning. He could still picture how the sunlight had streamed through her hair and danced across her magnificent skin, casting enticing highlights and shadows. It was as though his fingers could still feel the softness of her flesh and his lips taste the sweetness of her mouth. She fascinated and tantalized him and Tony wanted her more than he could remember ever wanting any woman.

But she had to be off limits to him. In the first place, he would be an idiot to return for more rejection. In the second, she was still what she was . . . a journalist out to make a fool of him. She'd tried to convince him the article would be flattering and beneficial to him, but he'd heard that line before. What was more, he couldn't forget that she'd already threatened to write the article anyway without his cooperation.

In a sudden spurt of anger, Tony's fist crashed down on his desk. Once a sports magazine writer had interviewed him, but he hadn't wanted to stick to the subject of football. He'd wanted more . . . and had gotten it. Innocently Tony had told him about living with his coach, Cal Borden and his wife, during his high school years. The reporter went to them, but when they refused to divulge anything of his earlier life, he went back to the old high school, found someone who knew he'd been raised in foster homes and from there had dug up the information about Tony's childhood . . . right down to the part where he'd once been in juvenile court for shoplifting at the age of nine. Naturally the truth behind that hadn't appeared in the story. Tony had been embarrassed beyond words by the article and from that time on he'd despised that reporter in particular and all reporters in general. But it was only after the same man harassed poor Danny Milstead that Tony had lost his cool and slugged the guy.

To this day Tony believed his teammate and friend, crushed enough by the burden of knowing one drunken evening behind a car wheel had cost an innocent person his life, had taken his own life later because he couldn't bear up under the pressure from the press. The sports magazine writer had been particularly obnoxious and aggressive and on the day of Danny's funeral, Tony, seeing the man at the cemetery, had blacked his eye when the service was over.

There had also been the three-ring circus that surrounded his court appearance when Carmen had tried to take him for a ride. The press had all but tried and hung him in the daily newspapers while they'd slanted their reports with lavish sympathetic overtones for her. Even when the suit had to be dismissed and it was proven that Carmen had tried to defraud him, they were lenient in their accounts of what happened, and her beautiful tear-stained face had appeared in newspapers around the country while she was quoted as being contrite yet defensive in her explanation that she'd only been doing the best she could for her child's future welfare.

Tony was brought out of his brooding thoughts by a discreet knock at his office door. It opened slowly and his secretary's head poked around the door. "Do you need anything else this afternoon, Mr. Neugent?"

Tony glanced at his watch, startled to see that it was nearing five. He shook his head. "No, go on home, Julie. I'll see you in the morning."

"All right." The girl added firmly, "Don't forget to pack your suitcase *and* bring your briefcase. If you intend to have the plane leave by ten tomorrow morning, I won't have time to drive out to Malibu for you."

He grinned and gave a mock salute. "Right, boss," he teased. He'd forgotten the last time he'd had to take a trip and Julie had wasted half the morning going to the house for his things.

After Julie left, Tony decided he might as well call it a day, too. He shrugged into his suit coat, flicked off the lights and left the office. When he stepped out of the elevator on the ground floor, he was taken aback to see Lisa standing in the small knot of people waiting to get into it.

His heart leapt at the sight of her. The crowd around them surged forward into the elevator. Others, spilling out from other elevators or first-floor offices, ebbed and flowed through the lobby, but Tony and Lisa were in a small world of their own. For a long time, they gazed wordlessly at each other and it seemed to Tony that she was as glad to see him as he was to see her.

But then he grew wary, and reminded himself not to be taken in by incredibly deep-green eyes and seductive pink lips. When he spoke, his voice was harsh even to his own ears. "I suppose you've come to gloat that you've dug up what dirt you could and have already sold your article about me?"

Chapter Six

Lisa flinched beneath his angry words and felt a keen disappointment. For one brief instant when they'd first looked at each other, she'd had the distinct impression that Tony had been happy to see her. Now she saw that his eyes were dark and remote and that his jaw was hard.

She shook her head and when she spoke her voice was husky. "No. That's . . . that's not what I came to say." Just then someone jostled her and she became aware that they were still blocking the entrance to the elevator and that the lobby had suddenly become jammed with people rushing to leave at the end of their work day. Lisa glanced around at the crowd, then looked back at Tony's tense face. "Is there someplace we can go that's a little more private?" she pleaded softly.

Tony looked at her as though he were making up his

mind whether to hear her out, and for a moment she feared he was going to refuse. But then he touched her elbow and guided her through the surging mass and out of the building into the late-afternoon sun.

When they paused on the sidewalk, he looked down at her, but the expression in his eyes was unreadable. "Where are you parked?" he asked.

Lisa managed a smile. "I don't have a car right now, remember? Jack had to go someplace nearby, so he was kind enough to give me a lift."

"I see," he replied. Again he touched her arm and led her around the side of the building and into the underground parking lot. When they reached his car, he opened the passenger door for her and Lisa slid inside. She wondered where he was taking her and almost asked, but given his obvious hesitation to talk to her at all, she decided it was wisest to remain silent.

Tony was quiet and seemed preoccupied as he maneuvered through the traffic. His office was in Beverly Hills and when he took the Santa Monica Freeway, Lisa assumed he was going to drive her back to her apartment. She decided she'd better say what she'd planned now, so she ventured, "Tony, I—"

"Not now," he interrupted without turning to look at her. "It'll keep, won't it, until we get home?"

"I suppose so," she agreed, "but Roni'll probably be home from work by the time we get there and—"

Again, Tony cut off her words and this time he did glance at her. "Not your home. Mine. Do you have any objections?"

Wordlessly, she shook her head. Tony returned his

attention to the freeway and Lisa was provided with an ample opportunity to observe him without his being acutely aware of it. The gray suit he wore was superbly cut. The jacket hugged his wide shoulders, displaying them to advantage. Her gaze traveled to his hands on the steering wheel. They were large hands with long, lithe fingers. Sensitive hands. Hands that could so quickly arouse her.

Abruptly curbing her wayward thoughts, Lisa looked down at her own tightly clasped hands. All week long she had hoped that Tony would telephone her. After all, they'd had a great time the evening he'd stayed to dinner at her apartment. She had hoped that maybe they could go from there and some sort of a relationship could evolve between them in a natural way. But he hadn't called, and with every passing day she had grown more depressed. She had thought of calling him, but then shrank from actually doing it. What could she have said, anyway? I'd like to see you? I think I'm falling in love with you? Impossible! While she'd had her share of boyfriends in her life, she'd never been so forward!

Still, it finally came to her that she would never hear from him again unless she made the first move, and when she realized why, she also knew it was her own fault. In her anger at his refusal to grant the interview she'd requested, she'd threatened to rehash old news reports about him and do a story anyway, and that had infuriated Tony. Since she'd actually read those accounts, it now made sense why he'd resented that so vehemently. He had been attracted to her since their first accidental meeting, but he'd had a week to think things over, to remember what she was and what she'd said she would do. Being honest with herself, Lisa had been forced to admit that if their positions were reversed, she wouldn't initiate any further meetings either. So in the end, she worked up the courage to approach him at his office this afternoon. No matter what the outcome, at least she would speak her piece.

When they reached Tony's oceanfront home in Malibu, he led her into a spacious living room in which the wall facing the beach was made entirely of glass. It revealed a roofed verandah and, beyond that, the beach and the endless stretch of the blue Pacific. The room itself was done in oyster-white, muted aqua colors and lots of glass and chrome. It was a beautiful place, at once luxurious yet casual and restful. It was a house that had definitely been planned for maximum comfort and enjoyment.

"It's wonderful," Lisa said half under her breath as she glanced around. "You must love living here!"

Tony shrugged. "I enjoy it," he admitted. He crossed the room to a built-in bar. "What would you like to drink?"

"Nothing."

He cocked his head to one side. "Nothing?"

Lisa glanced through the expansive glass panes once more and asked wistfully, "Would you mind terribly if we walked on the beach?"

Tony shrugged. "Why not? I keep forgetting you're a creature of the sea." His eyes moved from her face downward. She was wearing a soft green sundress and sandals, but her legs were bare. "Better take off your shoes," he advised as he shed his jacket and tie and unbuttoned the top two buttons on his shirt before rolling the sleeves to the elbows.

Lisa bent to slip off her shoes and her russet-gold hair spilled forward. Tony swallowed hard as he watched her easy, graceful movements. Why had she come to see him? he wondered. To continue the torture of making him want her? To remind him of her rejection?

With shoes off, Lisa stood straight and her gaze met . . . and locked with his. Though half the room separated them, Tony felt a strange impact as they looked at one another. Her wide emerald eyes seemed to invite him to drown in their depths, yet when she nervously moistened her lips, it was as though she were the one at risk. She appeared suddenly shy and uncertain, far different from the cool, self-assured young woman she'd been both when he'd first found her on the canyon road and the following afternoon when she'd presented herself at his ranch.

The moment ended when Lisa looked away. Tony went to the sliding glass door and opened it.

The afternoon sun was a circle of fire as it descended toward the ocean. The water was vivid blue streaked with flamboyant orange and pink. A few gulls squawked overhead as they headed away from the water's edge for their evening nests. The sand beneath their feet was still warm from the heat of the sunshine. A breeze ruffled and lifted Lisa's hair and Tony thought whimsically that the wind whistling across the water was singing just for her, offering a gentle love song created especially for a beautiful, mysterious mermaid from the sea. When she lifted her chin and inhaled deeply of the salty air and gazed with undisguised pleasure toward the water, it was almost easy to believe she was indeed as elemental as the natural forces surrounding them.

Even as he watched, her demeanor changed. All of a sudden, her face lost the rapt expression it had worn and her shoulders went rigid as though they were taking on a load of worldly cares. She glanced toward him and, when she found him watching her, quickly looked away again.

"I went to the library," she said without any particular inflection in her voice. "I read the things that have been written about you."

Tony clenched his teeth and he, too, stared off into the distance. Far down the beach he could see a lone figure walking. To their right were other beach houses, and as dusk began to fall there were lights in some of the windows, beckoning lights that seemed to denote peace and serenity. The turmoil inside of him was far from peaceful, however, and the security of his privacy was about to be invaded again. He knotted his fists at his side and struggled to control the anger that surged through him.

"Highly entertaining reading, wasn't it?" he said, unable to keep the bitterness from his voice. "So . . . when does your story hit the newsstands?"

"It doesn't." Lisa stopped in her tracks and looked at him. When she saw the tortured expression on his face, her throat tightened. She put out a hand to touch his arm, but Tony jerked away as though she had a contagious disease.

"Don't lie!" he grated. "You know very well it'll make an interesting story, a rehash of my past as a poor child shuffled around in foster homes who later made it big as a pro football star, then fought and won a paternity suit and still later donated a huge sum of money to disadvantaged children. It's the sort of soap opera the public loves. Did he give the money out of the goodness of his heart because of his own childhood or is it a way of appeasing his conscience because he won that court battle and maybe really is the father of that child? Your readers will have a great time raking me over the coals. I don't imagine you'll have the least bit of trouble selling such a story.''

"Neither do I," Lisa said, "if I were going to write it. *Today's Journal* wants it. But I won't, Tony. That's what I came to tell you.''

He looked at her for a long time without speaking. His eyes were piercing as he studied her face as though he could read the truth there. Finally, he sighed and shook his head as though he couldn't understand. "Why not?'' he asked simply.

Lisa shrugged and began to walk again. "It's just not the sort of information I'd care to use. I only wanted to write an informative, upbeat story about your generosity, not sensationalism. You've been kicked by the press enough already and I have no intention of repeating all that ancient history.''

This time Tony touched her arm, halting her slow progress along the almost deserted beach. "You have strange scruples for a journalist,'' he said bluntly.

Lisa grimaced. "I know. I'm not hard-nosed enough to ever make it good in this business.''

"But . . .'' Tony hesitated and Lisa thought he seemed

a little embarrassed before he finally blurted, "But don't
you need the money you'd make from the article?"

She laughed. "I *always* need money! That's nothing
new. And it's more than just the article itself. If I
delivered it, they were going to offer me a full-time job on
their staff."

"And you wanted it?"

"Desperately." The laughter faded and suddenly Lisa
was angry. Tony was certainly a hard man to convince.
"But I've told you I won't do the story," she said harshly,
"and I meant it. There are other subjects to write about
besides you, Mr. Anthony Neugent!"

Suddenly, Tony laughed. "I suppose there are, at that.
But what about the job?" he asked, turning serious. "I
had no idea something like that was involved, too."

Lisa shrugged. "There are other jobs."

Tony seemed to hesitate a moment and then he took a
step toward her. "I . . . Thanks, Lisa. I appreciate it a
lot." His eyes softened and his voice was low. "You've
got more kindness than any woman I've met for many
years."

There was a little catch in Lisa's throat as she teased,
"Then you've simply been meeting the wrong kind of
women."

"I think so, too," he agreed. "I just never thought
before to look for half-naked ones standing on the side of
the road and . . ."

He was suddenly talking to the air. Lisa took two steps
backward until she was in the water, bent and, cupping her
hands, scooped up water and tossed it in Tony's face.

With lightning speed, he sprang into action. Before Lisa could stand up straight, he was there; his powerful fingers were biting into her shoulders and, as she squealed in protest, he pushed her backward until she was completely immersed in the water. Then he came down, too, one strong thigh pinning her where she was while his hands captured hers.

"You're crazy!" Lisa gasped, laughing. She shook her wet head, trying to get the clumps of hair away from her face.

"I know." Tony grinned, released one of her hands and, with gentle fingers, pushed the hair away for her. "Crazy about you," he said huskily, just before he bent his head to claim her lips.

The water softly lapped over and around them as the two figures merged into one dark silhouette in the waning evening light. Gently rocked by the waves, it seemed as though the motion were a part of them, of the magic of the moment as they clung to each other.

Beneath the warm pressure of Tony's salty kisses, Lisa's lips parted, inviting him to taste, to explore, to find that which he was seeking.

Their wet clothing molded to their bodies, leaving them covered but not concealed. Tony's hand brushed against Lisa's breast and she shivered in reaction. A streak of fire flashed through her and involuntarily, she pressed her body tighter to his.

Her movement seemed to inflame Tony. His mouth released hers and for an endless moment they gazed at each other. Rising passion smoldered in his dark eyes as they swept over her face. Then he bent his head once more and his lips found the sensitive hollow of her throat.

Tony ran one hand along the length of her exposed leg and Lisa gasped as it trailed up her thigh. Her blood raced madly, pounding like thunderous waves through her veins. Never had she been so intimately aware of a man, so acutely sensitive to his every touch.

Her arms slipped around him, stroking his muscular back. His shirt, thin though it was, offended her and she tugged at it until her fingertips could feel his slick, wet flesh beneath them.

Tony shifted his position so that the length of him was more closely molded to hers. Lisa was breathless as she felt his desire, hard and strong, throbbing against her. His hand slid up to hold the weight of her breast in his palm and her senses whirled. She was braless beneath the dress and now her nipples grew taut and strained against the bodice.

Then, Tony's hands stilled. He lifted his head, halting the disturbing plundering of her emotions. He looked deeply into her eyes, his breathing as raspy as hers was erratic.

Lisa almost cried out in protest. Her mind had been floating on a haze of pleasurable sensations and now it had stopped. Aroused and abruptly frustrated, she looked blankly at Tony, not understanding. Then the mists cleared and she saw clearly the question that burned in his gaze. The outline of his face was hard and chiseled, betraying his tension. Mutely, he was asking her to make her decision. Was she going to draw back a second time,

to forbid once more the release they both so desperately
needed?

There was something endearing in that look and Lisa
saw what she had not noticed that afternoon by the stream.
Tony might be a wealthy, successful, even famous man,
but he was as susceptible to the pain of rejection as anyone
else. In that instant she recognized that while he wanted
her physically, it also went deeper than that for him, just
as it did for her.

She didn't dare stop to consider the wisdom of what she
was doing. If she did, she knew she'd find a thousand
reasons why she should end this madness now. But she
didn't want it to end, not without fulfillment for them
both. Caution, after all, was for the cowardly.

Boldly, seductively and with full cognizance of what
she was doing, Lisa smiled and slowly wound her arms
around Tony's neck. Pulling him close, she pressed her
body to his and placed her lips on his firm mouth.

It was a searing kiss, stunning them both by its
powerful effect upon them. It alternately demanded and
yielded, sought and found, was gentle and violent, and
each of them were by turns possessed and the possesser.
Tony, after his initial surprise by her action, crushed his
arms around her, holding her so closely that they seemed
to share a single heartbeat. Lisa felt as though she were
whirling in dizzying spirals of growing passion. She
wondered faintly how long it could possibly continue
before a person died of the wanting.

Tony dragged his mouth from hers at last and his eyes
were glazed with an unmistakable hunger. His voice was

slow and thick as he asked, "Are you sure this time? Really sure?"

Even now he was giving her the chance to back out. But Lisa's own need was far too great. She trembled with a dreadful aching that seemed to have no end. "I'm sure," she said huskily.

Abruptly, Tony stood. Seawater poured off them both as he lifted Lisa into his arms. For an instant they gazed at each other in wondrous silence as he held her. Then Lisa nestled her wet head beneath his chin and tightened her clasp around his neck as he carried her to shore. Never had she felt more as though she belonged, that this was the place to be, the right place. She was as certain of it as she was that the world was round, that the sun always set in the west, that the moon controlled the tides. It was a given, an absolute, and she was content.

Tony carried her across the soft sand, up the stairs to the verandah and into his house. Pausing only long enough to allow Lisa to reach out and close and latch the sliding glass door, he then took her into his bedroom where he placed her gently on the bed.

"Oh, no," she protested weakly. "Tony, we're so wet! The bed . . ."

"Forget the bed," Tony growled as he came down beside her. "Concentrate on this instead." He gathered her into his arms and the kiss he gave her made her forget her objections.

Moments later he half lifted her and helped her out of the soggy dress. It fell with a dull thud to the carpet as Tony's attention became riveted to Lisa.

She lay quite still, a little shy, while his gaze traveled down the entire length of her body. Nothing was concealed from his vision except where the small, triangular scrap of lacy fabric wrapped itself around her lower hips.

In a flash, that, too, was gone, and Tony's eyes narrowed as they feasted on the captivating beauty of her soft, peach-colored skin. Her perfection was breathtaking, from the delicate fan of her thick eyelashes right down to her toes. Her breasts were full and firm, cresting to shell-pink tips; she had the tiniest of waists. He was sure he could place both his hands around it and have his fingers meet. Her hips were smooth and rounded with tantalizing curves and her legs were long and shapely. The place where her thighs met was so lovely the sight rocked his equilibrium.

"You are," he whispered unsteadily, "magnificent." His hand moved to gently caress a breast before he bent his head to touch it with his mouth.

Lisa's throat ached. His tongue teased her nipple, playfully etching moist circles around it. The agonizing frenzy that shot through her became intolerable and she pressed her fingers hard into his shoulders, clinging as best she could to some semblance of reality.

Tony's fiery kisses moved down to burn the flat valley of her midsection and Lisa was fast leaving coherent thought behind. Then, abruptly, he moved away and his dark gaze glittered as he quickly peeled away his own wet clothes.

Lisa's pulse quickened as she watched him. His tall, solid frame carried not an ounce of spare flesh. Powerful muscles ebbed and flowed beneath his bronzed skin, according to his movements. His shoulders were straight and broad as befitted an athlete and the strength that was evident in his arms and hands might have been alarming if she hadn't already discovered that the strength was tempered with gentleness. His torso narrowed toward his waist and a dark jungle of hair matted the center of his chest. Below narrow hips bulged powerful thighs. A flutter of intense hunger shook her, and, surrendering to it, she opened her arms in welcome as he came back to her.

Tony's lovemaking tapped depths Lisa had never even suspected she had. There seemed no part of her he forgot as he kissed her, caressed her, aroused her to unbelievable heights. Her bones melted as he held dominion over her raw, quivering emotions. It was as though until this night she had been an unfurled flower, a tightly closed bud that was now spreading open with joyous ecstasy beneath the gloriously warm rays of the sun.

Lisa allowed the savage sensations to run riot as she, in turn, savored with intense delight the unfamiliar and heady pleasure of lifting Tony to the same frenzied excitement. She threaded her fingers through his hair, then trailed her fingertips down to knead his smooth back. She nibbled at his earlobes before dropping tiny kisses on his throat and then down his chest. Sensuously, dangerously bold, she played tattoos along his hips and legs as her hair brushed his skin with feather-light flirtation.

All at once, the games were over. Tony sucked in a sharp breath, as though he had reached the limit of his endurance and he fitted her to the angular contours of his body. Lisa was as ready as he and she arched toward him with eager anticipation.

And then they were together, moving in blissful unison to the tempo of love. Ever higher they climbed until the rarefied heights were overwhelming. Lisa gasped and she faintly heard the sounds of Tony's heavy breathing as they neared the pinnacle and then, in a rapturous explosion, scaled it.

Lisa felt Tony shudder even as she trembled. For a long moment they clung together more tightly as the aftershocks rumbled through them. Little by little the assaults faded, until finally they were still.

Then Tony moved, shifting his weight from her to the bed. Their eyes met, soft and happy, and they smiled at each other. Tony reached over to trace her lips with his forefinger before he bent to kiss her.

"Darling," he whispered. "Oh, my darling. After that, I don't plan to ever let you go."

"So who wants to go anywhere?" she teased gently as her hands slid up to his shoulders.

Tony sighed contentedly. "I knew I wanted you from the first moment I saw you standing by your car wearing that outlandish costume."

Lisa playfully slapped his shoulder. "You're never going to let me forget that night, are you?"

"Never," Tony said with a twinkle in his eyes. "It's not every day a man meets the girl of his dreams like that."

Girl of his dreams! How she hoped he meant it! Still, something inside warned her not to take it too literally just yet. She strove for the light touch. "Hmmm, as I recall, you didn't seem to like me very much at the time."

Tony grinned. "Of course I did. Enough so that I didn't want you running around in public dressed like that when any man could—" He broke off. "And besides, I was busy enough trying to keep my mind off you myself. Later, when I saw you at the party, I was so damned jealous of every other man there who paid attention to you that I wanted to break their faces and strangle you for putting me through such torture in the first place! I hated them looking at you."

He looked so ferocious that in spite of caution Lisa was beginning to believe him. She sighed. "I hated it, too, believe me. I didn't know when I first got signed for the commercial that the costume would be quite so revealing. Then, for that party, Dusty flatly ordered us to show up and do the routine as a surprise for Mr. Gate. I thought I'd be able to just do the song and dance and leave right afterward. I hadn't counted on having to stay and mingle with the guests. Or," she added with a little laugh, "being glared at all evening by you! You made me absolutely livid!"

"Aha!" Tony's eyes glinted triumphantly. "At least you weren't indifferent to me."

"No, that I wasn't. I was still fuming about you the next day when I drove up to the ranch. I can't tell you how horrified I was to see you there!"

Tony chuckled. "I can't say I was very happy to see you either. In the first place I hadn't liked finding myself interested in you; in the second, my ranch is off limits to all the women I know and I was furious that you'd have the nerve to follow me there, and then when I found out who you really were, I had to fight myself not to physically throw you off the place.''

''Instead you had to put me up.'' Lisa aligned her fingers with his, noting with fascinated interest how much longer his fingers were than hers.

Tony closed his hand around hers, lifted her fingertips to his lips and kissed them one by one. His eyes were slumberous and filled with contentment as he gazed at her. ''I have to say I enjoyed that much more than I'd anticipated.'' His voice became serious. ''I wanted to call you all this week, Lisa. But I just couldn't. I knew you'd look up those old stories about me and I thought you'd do that article over my objections like you'd threatened. No matter how much I'd begun to care for you, that kept getting in the way.''

''I know,'' she said earnestly. ''I kept hoping you'd call and when you didn't, I finally realized you never would as long as you thought I'd use that information. That's why I went to your office today.''

''God knows it shouldn't bother me.'' He laughed roughly. ''After all, it's nothing that hasn't been printed already for all the world to see. But it does. I guess I've become a fanatic about privacy. I'm really glad you decided not to write that stuff over again. And I'm deeply glad you came to me today.''

''So am I,'' Lisa said softly.

They took showers, and while Tony cooked steaks, Lisa perched on a bar stool and watched him, once again dressed in his robe while her clothes were running through the washer and dryer. They laughed reminiscently about that, remembering that stormy afternoon at the ranch. In fact, they laughed about a lot of things that evening. Their discussion ran the gamut from politics to Lisa's parents to college courses they had taken.

They had their dinner at a low glass table in the living room where they sat informally on throw pillows on the floor. Afterward, sipping wine, they leaned against the soft, plush sofa and relaxed.

Tony caught Lisa's hand in his and smiled. "I don't want to see this evening end."

Lisa returned the smile. "Neither do I. But there's always tomorrow. Isn't there?"

Tony squeezed her hand and shook his head. "I wish there were, but I'm leaving in the morning on a business trip. Dallas first, then Atlanta and New York."

Lisa couldn't hide her disappointment. "How long will you be away?"

"About ten days. I wish," he murmured as he leaned forward to brush her lips with a light kiss, "that I didn't have to go."

"I wish you didn't, too," Lisa said unhappily.

"Come with me," Tony said abruptly. "I'm serious," he insisted when she looked surprised. "I don't want to leave you."

Lisa smiled ruefully. "You tempt me," she said truthfully. "But I can't. I've got a couple of interviews lined up next week for articles that have already been approved."

Tony wrinkled his nose. "You told me I wasn't the only subject to write about and you meant it, didn't you?"

Lisa laughed at him. "What's the matter now, Mr.

Neugent?'' she teased. "Was that a blow to your ego? Want to change your mind about the interview after all?''

Tony grinned. "It might almost be worth it . . . if I could convince you to come with me. Can't you postpone your interviews?''

Lisa became serious. "I suppose I could, but I won't. You'll be busy most of the time while you're gone, Tony, and I'd just be hanging around waiting for you. Besides, maybe this will be good for us. Maybe we need a breather, a little time apart, a chance to think.''

"About how serious this is getting?'' He was no longer laughing either.

She nodded.

"Maybe you're right,'' Tony said speculatively. "I've never felt the least urge to invite a woman on a trip with me before. I never thought I'd miss anyone that much.''

"I never wanted to accept such an invitation before, either,'' she said, smiling.

Tony looked deeply into her eyes. "Are we in love?''

"I don't know,'' she said quietly. "Are we?''

"When I come back, we'll definitely have to find out. Okay if I call you every night while I'm away?''

"I'll be devastated if you don't,'' Lisa told him, putting her vulnerability on the line.

Tony smiled, content, then tugged at her hand. "Come help me pack?'' he asked.

It was nearing eleven when Tony drove Lisa back to her own apartment. They got out of the car and strolled leisurely toward the stairs, hand in hand, each of them reluctant to end the evening, dreading the long parting that was to come.

When they reached the foot of the stairway that lead up to her apartment, they paused.

"I don't want to say good-bye," Tony said huskily. "I think—"

A figure suddenly stepped out of the dark shadows near the building. "Lisa!" a masculine voice exclaimed. "Darling, where have you been? I've been waiting for you all evening!" He moved onto the lighted sidewalk and added, "Come on upstairs, baby. We've got wedding plans to discuss."

Lisa was so stunned that all she could do was stare at the man. He moved beside her and slid his arm possessively around her waist.

When she looked up, she saw that Tony was as taken aback as she was. But then a forbidding expression came to his face, and his eyes, when they met hers for one eternity of a moment, burned her with his contempt. Before she could form a coherent thought or utter a word of explanation, he walked swiftly away, got into his car and drove off.

Chapter Seven

*L*isa watched Tony drive away with the most profound feeling of helplessness and dismay she could ever recall. It was as though he were taking some vital essence of herself with him, something she would never be able to recapture.

When he was out of sight, she rounded on Kevin like a wildcat. "I hate you for this!" she exclaimed.

Kevin Dyer's smooth face crinkled as he grinned unrepentantly. "Of course you don't. I only spoke the truth and I just figured it was the quickest way to get rid of whoever he is. He's not important anyway, sweetheart. We are." He reached for her, but Lisa neatly sidestepped his outstretched hands.

"Have you lost your mind or have I?" she asked sarcastically. "I could have sworn you said something about wedding plans and we both know you're highly allergic to marriage."

"Not anymore. These last couple of months without you have made me change my mind. I really mean it, Lisa," he added when he saw her skeptical expression. "Listen, my company has given me a promotion and in three weeks I'm being transferred to St. Louis. I think we should get married. I want you to come with me."

Lisa gazed into the handsome face of the man she had once deluded herself into thinking she loved. It was a weak, self-indulgent face, she saw now, and she wondered why it had taken her so long to realize that. She supposed when she'd first begun to date him she'd been a little enthralled by his good looks, the teasing blue eyes and easy smile. Also, Kevin could be utterly charming when he wanted to be and she'd had some good times going out with him. But their relationship had quickly soured when he'd wanted her to move in with him and she had refused. He'd made a big deal about how well they could live if they pooled their finances and insisted it made good sense because she'd be needing to find a new roommate in a few months anyway, once Roni married. When she'd still obstinately vetoed the idea, Kevin had become incensed. He'd sworn he loved her but said she was cheapening their love by trying to trap him into a marriage before he was ready.

Lisa had never dreamed of trapping any man into marriage. Someday she hoped to marry and have a family, but when it happened she wanted the man to be as eager for it as she was. Something deep inside warned her that Kevin's reluctance to make a real commitment wasn't likely to change in the future and that she would be very foolish to fall in with his wishes. Besides, she hadn't been all that sure that she loved him enough to carry their relationship that one step further.

Even so, she had been very unhappy for quite some time over their breakup. Life had seemed flat and dull without him. But one day she had realized that while she missed the fun-loving Kevin, she didn't miss the irresponsible one. Even if he had offered marriage, it would have been a mistake. With Kevin, a girl would always have to worry about money, because it ran through his hands like water, and worst of all, she'd have to worry about other women, because flirting was as much a part of his nature as breathing.

She shook her head. "Sorry, Kevin, but I'm just not interested anymore." She stepped past him toward the stairs.

"Look, what is it you want of me?" he asked harshly. "I'm giving in to what you want. I'm willing to marry you. Lisa, I miss you and I want you to go with me."

Lisa paused with one foot on the bottom stair and she turned back to him. "You're *willing* to marry me?" she asked incredulously. "Anyone would think you were forced to come here tonight and say that! What's the matter, Kevin? Is it that you're dreading going to a new city where you don't know anyone or does your company have a new policy against single men? You don't love me, not really. You never did. If you had, you'd have wanted to marry me, not just been willing to!"

"I do love you," he insisted. "And all right, I *want* to marry you. So now can you stop being angry with me and just say 'yes'?"

"I can't. You see, I just don't love you. So it would have been a mistake either way for us, whether we'd just lived together or gotten married. Good luck in your new position. And good-bye."

"Is it the man who just left?" Kevin asked swiftly. "Do you love him?"

"Yes," she said firmly, very definite in her own mind now. "Yes, I do. Though I may never be able to convince him of that after the little bomb you dropped tonight."

Kevin looked at her silently for a time. "I guess there's nothing more for us to talk about, then, is there?" he asked unhappily.

"No, I don't think so," she agreed quietly.

When Lisa got upstairs to the apartment, she tried to call Tony, but he didn't answer. Despondent, she got undressed and ready for bed and then she tried again, with no results. She kept trying until almost one o'clock, but then she gave up in defeat. Either Tony had not gone back home for the night or he simply wasn't answering his phone.

She could understand his anger over Kevin's unexpected appearance and startling announcement, but surely once he cooled down he would realize that she'd been just as startled as he and would ask her for an explanation before leaping to any conclusions.

But during the next week and a half, she finally had to

admit to herself that he had no intention of asking. He'd promised to call her while he was out of town, but it was a call that never came.

There was no question in Lisa's mind anymore about whether she loved Tony. It was absurd and flew in the face of all reason to fall so quickly in love, especially with a man she'd known for such a short while, yet she had— overwhelmingly, deeply, irrevocably. She'd suspected it after the weekend at his ranch, but since the evening at his beach house she'd known for certain. She'd welcomed his lovemaking because for her it had been an honest expression of that love.

She'd never felt this way about any man before. While she had enjoyed going out with Kevin, she had never been concerned over the lack of depth between them; and while she'd missed him after they'd split up, she had always known that it was not her heart but her pride that had been affected. But what she felt for Tony was so different from what she'd felt for Kevin that it was almost like trying to compare a first-year art student's work with the genius of Picasso. There was no comparison. For Tony she wanted everything, success, health and whatever would bring him happiness, and she felt deep regret that after the things they'd said to each other that night, he'd been hurt and angered by Kevin's unexpected visit. She wished with all her being that she'd been able to reach him by phone before he'd left on his trip to tell him it wasn't what he'd thought.

If the nights were unbearably lonely while she waited for the telephone to ring, at least the days were filled. Lisa kept busy with her interviews and writing. She worked long hours and with a fervor that surprised even herself, especially since she had little enthusiasm for the subject matter. One article was about a woman and her show dogs for a pet magazine; another was about a man who had made a fortune on the stock market, yet continued his job as a fireman because he loved it. She spoke by phone with a couple of editors concerning future projects and went out to lunch with friends. But despite all the frenzied activity, her thoughts were never far from Tony or the days remaining until he returned.

On the day he'd planned to be back, Lisa telephoned his office. His secretary took her name, promising to have him return her call, but he never did. In the evening, she called the Malibu house, but though she kept trying until well past midnight, Tony never answered it. She repeated the entire process the next day, again with no success, and finally she had to acknowledge to herself that he had no intention of speaking to her.

The following day she received the check from the television commercial she'd done. It meant that now she could afford to get her car repaired, but that presented a new problem. In order to retrieve the car, she had to get in touch with Tony. He kept the entrance gate to the ranch locked when he was away and she had to get onto the property. But now that he'd made it so clear that he didn't want to talk to her, she shrank from the necessity of it. She also wondered how she was even going to manage it since he never returned any of her calls.

Tony rubbed his hands wearily across his eyes, then focused them once more on the small print of the contract he was reading. It was late Friday afternoon, it had been a long day and he was so tired that the words either kept blurring together or became meaningless to him.

In irritation he shoved the papers to one side of the desk, then reached for the small sheet of paper near the phone. "While you were out," the printed message read, and beside it, in Julie's precise handwriting, were the words "Lisa Knight called . . . twice."

Tony stared at the paper and frowned. Why didn't she just leave him in peace? he wondered. Surely the fact that he hadn't returned any of her calls these past three days ought to tell her plainly enough that he didn't want to talk to her. What the hell did she expect him to say, anyway? Congratulations! When's the wedding? He couldn't do it. He wasn't that magnanimous, wasn't that casual and easygoing.

Damn her anyway, he thought savagely. What kind of person was she to let him make love to her while she was planning to marry someone else? Answer: just like Carmen, selfish and cruel . . . a heartless cheat. And he'd been fool enough to think they had something special, that he was falling in love with her! Pain spewed through his veins, raw and burning. Tony crumpled the scrap of paper in his hand and tossed it across the room.

Knowing he wasn't going to get anymore work done today, he heaved himself to his feet. In the outer office, Julie was still at work. Tony struggled to conceal the violent emotions that seethed within him.

"I'm leaving, Julie. I may go up to the ranch for the weekend and if I do, I probably won't be back until

Monday morning sometime. If I'm not here by nine, call Morley and postpone our meeting."

"Yes, sir. Have a nice weekend."

Tony laughed mirthlessly to himself. Sure, he was bound to have a terrific weekend struggling to forget the girl who had so quickly come to mean so much to him. Why couldn't he stop thinking about the pleasant sound of her voice, the appeal of her quick smile, the soft silkiness of her body when he'd held her? All he'd been doing for almost two long weeks now was torturing himself with his ungovernable thoughts.

Lisa was on edge, anxious and filled with dread as she drove Roni's car toward Malibu. He mightn't be there, of course, and all her worry would have been for nothing, because just before she'd left the apartment she'd tried once more to phone his house and, like all the other times, Tony hadn't answered. Yet even if he wasn't home, the confrontation wouldn't be canceled; it would only be postponed. Sometime soon, she had to see him. She needed her car and surely he couldn't object to her borrowing his key so she could go up to get it.

Still, she didn't look forward to seeing him, not anymore, not since all this time had passed and he'd made it plain he wanted nothing more to do with her.

When she reached his house, her level of panic rose and her heart began to pound in her throat. There were lights gleaming from the windows. He *was* home. She had to beat down the urge to simply go away again without his ever knowing she had come. Lisa took a long, ragged breath and, finally, got out of the car and walked to the front door on rubbery legs.

After she rang the bell there was an agonizingly long wait. Her mouth went dry and her breathing became erratic. She had just decided he wasn't home after all and was turning away when she heard the scrape of the lock and, suddenly, light spilled over her.

Lisa's blood raced swift and hot at the sight of him. He'd obviously just stepped out of the shower. He wore the same brown robe she'd twice worn herself and a thick white towel hung around his neck. A small rivulet of water ran down his right cheek. His appearance was at once exciting and disturbing. She was extremely aware of his virile sexuality, of the gap down the center of his chest which the robe did not cover, of the fresh, soap-clean scent about him and most of all, of that which she couldn't see except in her mind's eye, the part of him that was concealed by the dark fabric.

For a long time they only stared at each other. The tension wrapped itself around them, invisible, but very real, binding them so that neither could seem to move or speak. Tony's face was partially shadowed because of the light behind him, giving dark, harsh angles to the planes of his face.

He spoke at last and his words were sarcastic and derisive. "You're persistent, if nothing else. I'll at least give you that."

"Please." Lisa's voice was a bit unsteady and it held a pleading quality. "Don't be like that. I have to talk to you."

"I doubt if I'd be interested in whatever you have to say."

Lisa swallowed hard and tried again. "Will you let me come in or do we have to conduct our conversation out here?"

"It doesn't matter to me one way or the other," he replied indifferently. "But as long as you're here, I guess you can come in if that's what you want." He stepped aside so that she could enter the house.

In the living room they faced each other, stiff and wary. Tony's stance was belligerent. His bare feet were planted far apart, his arms were crossed and his head was tilted to one side in an impatient gesture. His lips were pressed firmly together. Hostility emanated from him, cold and unyielding.

Lisa was more intimidated by his manner than she'd expected to be and it threw her off-balance. She forgot everything except his anger and she almost cried out in protest.

"You got your way," Tony said in a voice as cold as ice water. "You're here, so now say whatever you came to say and get out of my house."

Lisa's chin went up and soft color stained her cheeks. "It won't take long," she said in a rush. "I'd like to get my car tomorrow, but I'll need to borrow your key so the garage's tow truck will be able to get through the gate."

"That won't be necessary," Tony said. "I'll be there myself, so you won't have any trouble getting in."

"I . . . see." Lisa inhaled a shuddering breath and fought off tears. It was impossible to say the rest of what she'd planned to say. Tony was in no mood to listen and matters could only get worse if she tried. "That's fine. I'll be going, then."

She took a couple of steps toward the entrance of the room. There was no choice but to go around Tony, but when she tried, his hands shot out and clasped her arms.

His hold was punishing and Lisa winced from the unexpected pain. Her eyes lifted to his face and she saw livid anger there just before he jerked her roughly against him and his mouth assaulted hers.

There was no gentleness, no caring in the kiss. His mouth was hard and cruel on hers. Lisa felt as though she were being suffocated by it, and in automatic self-defense she beat against his chest with knotted fists.

But Tony's strength made the gesture futile. She might as well have been hammering at the thick metal walls of a vault at Fort Knox for all the effect she had upon him and in that moment she was afraid.

As though he sensed it, his demeanor suddenly altered. His own hands inched up between them to capture hers and though they were firm as they wrapped securely around her fingers and ended her attack, they were no longer cruel. They were warm, almost comforting, and at the same time the pressure of his kiss decreased.

Lisa stilled, believing he was about to release her. But he did not. Instead, his mouth moved softly over hers, caressing, then playful and finally, to her utter confusion, with the unmistakable signs of passion. The kiss became urgent and forceful as it parted her lips. A floodtide of desire, shocking in its wide sweep, deluged her as his tongue darted between her teeth. The sensual intimacy carried away all her resistance, leaving instead a tumultuous current of intense need. Her mind swirled as her body weakened with desperate craving.

Tony's hands released hers and moved up to her shoulders, pulling her closer to him. Then they slid slowly down her back, following its curve to her hips. His mouth abruptly abandoned her lips in favor of the hollow at her throat, and beneath his warm moist breath she could feel her pulse skip a beat.

Lisa gasped softly and her skin, growing flushed and warm, tingled in reaction to his stirring kisses at the sensitive spot. The tip of her breasts brushed his chest and the fleeting contact added to the havoc that had already destroyed her self-composure. Giddy and needing to cling to his solid form to support herself, she clasped her hands around his neck.

Tony's kisses traveled upward from her throat, along the outline of her jaw to her earlobe while his hands tugged her blouse free of her skirt. Then his fingers moved beneath it and his thumb rubbed in a semicircular motion across her midsection before going at last to touch the soft contours of her breast. Lisa's breath caught and she swayed against him.

Suddenly Tony was pulling her down, his persuasive hands drawing her to the floor. Weakened by the protracted assault on her senses, she could not have fought the action had she wanted to.

Tony reached to the sofa for a throw pillow, then pressed Lisa down until her head was on it. His robe gaped open, revealing the wide expanse of his bare chest, and the sight of it was enticing to her. Her hands went to it, running gently from his throat toward his waist across the crisp, wiry black hair.

He allowed her to have her way for a few moments, but then made her stop so that he could unbutton her blouse. He half lifted her to help her out of it and then unhooked her bra and tossed it aside. His gaze lowered to her breasts and it seared her with its burning intensity.

Slowly, he bent over her and while his hand caressed one breast, his mouth sought the other.

His lips teasing the aroused peaks of her nipples set Lisa on fire. Her hands returned to his muscular chest, raking it with her fingernails as the fervent tempo of her desire became a demanding compulsion.

"Not enough," she murmured as the sweet torture of his teeth nibbling at her nipples sent her crazy. "Not enough! Please, Tony!" Blindly, she clawed at the folds of his robe, trying to get rid of its bulky interference. Her whole body arched toward him, straining for release. Her lower limbs were numb with a desperate ache.

Tony lifted his head. His eyes were hooded and his face was tense from his own emotions. "Tell me you want me," he commanded huskily.

"I want you," she whispered.

"Tell me you want me more than anyone in the world."

"I do. I . . ." She stopped and stared at him blankly, not comprehending as he moved away from her. Her body was suddenly cold where his hands had been and her heart leapt to her throat, clogging it as though there was a lump of solid ice in it as she watched a slow grin spread across his face. "Tony?" she ended weakly.

Tony got to his feet and pulled his robe more securely

about him. "That's all I wanted to hear," he said flatly. "Now you can get dressed and leave."

"I . . . I don't understand," she stammered. Lisa sat upright and pulled her blouse to her front to shield her bareness.

"Give it some thought," Tony said harshly, "and I'm sure you will."

"There can be no other reason than that you wanted to make a fool of me," she said in a subdued voice.

Tony nodded. Lisa went so pale that for an instant he felt ashamed of what he'd done. But then he reminded himself of all that had gone before and he hardened his heart. "You didn't mind rejecting me that afternoon at the ranch. And then that other night"—his voice broke off and he sucked in a deep breath—"you came to me all right, only to rush back to your fiancé's waiting arms! What kind of a fool is he, Lisa, that he'll take you in spite of your cheating? And what kind of woman are you to do it in the first place?"

Lisa visibly shivered and even seemed to shrink in size as she lowered her head, fighting tears. Against his will, Tony was struck by her defenselessness beneath his verbal attack and, insanely, he felt a wild urge to gather her into his arms and comfort her.

But almost instantly she changed. She got to her feet and her gaze was scornful as it swept over his face. "What kind of woman am I?" she repeated in a choked, angry voice. "Obviously a lousy judge of character to have ever had anything to do with you at all!"

She turned her back to him and struggled into her bra and then her blouse. Tony's eyes fixed on the copper curls that swished against her shoulders, but he really wasn't seeing. A perplexed frown wrinkled his forehead. He could understand her being angry and resentful after the nasty trick he'd just played, but where did she get off casting aspersions on *his* character?

"I may not be a saint," he snapped, "but you sure as hell aren't either!"

Fully dressed, Lisa turned to face him. Every line in her body was stiff with anger and her voice, when she spoke, was thick with unshed tears. Yet, at the same time, there was a certain dignity and poise to her bearing that was as impressive as it was unexpected.

"I never claimed to be a saint," she said in a soft, restrained tone. "But one thing I can tell you. I've never deliberately set out to harm or shame someone in all my life the way you just did. I may make mistakes, but at least I have a conscience."

Tony's eyes glittered with fire and he uttered a harsh, gritty sound that passed for a humorless laugh. "Save it for your fiancé. Maybe he'll buy your pious words! I sure don't. Now go! I'm sure he's waiting for you, expecting to have another laugh over the way you put down Tony Neugent. By the looks of it, the two of you are perfectly matched. You deserve each other!"

To Tony's amazement, Lisa flinched and he saw that her hands were shaking. She sucked in a deep breath and then met his gaze fully, and there was no hint of apology in the depths of her eyes.

"You're warped, you know that? Because of one bad experience with a woman, you've let it color your logic. If you ever had any, that is!'' She shook her head before adding, ''I really feel sorry for you, Tony. You don't know how to care about anything or anybody except your own damn pride!''

A dull flush came to his face and with it, overwhelming bitterness. ''I don't want your pity,'' he grated as he struggled to control the surge of anger rolling over him like the undulating waves of a California earthquake. ''I don't want anything from you at all except never to see you again! You disgust me!''

He saw pain streak across her face. The color in her cheeks drained away, her green eyes took on the shade of jade, dull and smoky, and her shoulders suddenly slumped as though in absolute defeat. The fight in her had gone.

Lisa moved toward the door, passing so close to him that if he'd wanted, he could have reached out to touch her. But he didn't. In silence, he watched her go.

But when she reached the doorway, she surprised him by turning toward him once more. Tony braced himself, expecting her to lash out at him with more hurtful words. Instead, he saw tears shimmering in the depths of her eyes and her voice was husky and sad.

''I'm going,'' she assured him. ''And once my car is off your property, I'll be out of your life. But so you won't remember me quite so badly, I want you to know the truth. Kevin is a man I used to date, but when he showed up that evening, I hadn't seen him for two months. He asked me to marry him that night and I refused. I tried to call you afterward to explain, but you didn't answer your telephone. Nor would you take any of my calls since you came back from your trip. I never''—her voice thickened —''did anything to make a fool of you. I cared too much.''

She turned and walked through the hall toward the door.

For a fraction of a minute, Tony was paralyzed with shock. Then wild hope surged through him and he rushed after her. Lisa's hand was on the doorknob, but before she could turn it, he was there.

He gripped her arm. ''Is this . . . true?'' His voice was urgent and ragged with emotion.

''Of course.'' Lisa shook his hand away from her arm and opened the door. ''I told you once I'm not a liar. I'm not a cheat, either.'' She stepped toward the door.

''Stay,'' Tony insisted. ''Lisa, let me apologize!''

''It's too late for that,'' she said in a dull, flat voice. ''You refused to give me the benefit of the doubt. This isn't the first time you've made snap judgments about me. It seems that no matter what I do, as far as you're concerned, it's suspect.'' She shrugged lightly. ''I don't need that from you or anyone else! I'd like to say it's been nice knowing you, but it hasn't.'' Whirling around, she ran out of the house into the dark night.

Tony followed, but when he reached her car, she was already inside it. ''Please don't go,'' he begged through the partially opened window. ''Let's talk things over sensibly and—''

''We've done all the talking I ever care to do,'' Lisa said gruffly. ''Good-bye, Tony.''

She shifted into reverse and the car began to move. Feeling impotent and helpless, Tony stepped back and shoved his knotted fists into the pockets of his robe. He watched until the red taillights of the car disappeared through the gate and then he cursed himself viciously.

What an appalling mess he'd made of things! He had permanently alienated the only person in the world who mattered to him and all because of his stupid pride. He'd set out to make her hate him, and heaven help him, he'd certainly done a terrific job of it!

Tony went back into the house and violently slammed the front door behind him. But the satisfaction of releasing his fury at himself was only a momentary, fleeting thing. He returned to the living room and sank into a chair. Then he hunched over, arms on his knees, and covered his face with his hands. He had never felt more bereft in his life.

Chapter Eight

By the time Lisa reached home, she was shivering with chills just as badly as when she'd had a virus last winter. In fact, she did feel quite ill. Her stomach was twisted into a knot and her face felt flushed.

She was surprised to find Roni there when she let herself into the apartment. Comfortably ensconced on the sofa, she wore pajamas and was painting her toenails while she watched a television program.

"I thought you said you were going out with Jack tonight. Why are you in so early?"

"He called me right after you left. His younger brother was involved in a motorcycle accident. He's gone to San Diego to be with his parents."

"How dreadful!" Lisa exclaimed. "Is he badly hurt?"

"They're really not sure yet. But Jack said his dad sounded terribly upset, so he thought he should go and be with them."

"Well, certainly." Lisa sat down at the opposite end of the sofa. "Why didn't you go with him?" She knew Roni had a very good relationship with Jack's family.

"Because I have to go into the office and work a couple of hours tomorrow morning. But as soon as I'm finished, I'll be heading out of town." For the first time she really looked at Lisa. "You don't look so well yourself. Are you all right?"

Lisa shook her head. "No. Actually, I'm falling apart at the seams."

"You saw Tony?"

"I saw him all right," Lisa said bitterly. "And he made a complete fool of me."

Roni looked interested. "What happened?"

"He . . . he started kissing me, started making love to me. When he was sure I really wanted him, he told me to get out. He deliberately humiliated me, Roni!" She looked away and her lips trembled as she struggled for control.

"Surely you're imagining things," Roni said, trying to soothe her. "Tony seemed like a pretty nice person when I met him. I can't even visualize him doing something that cruel."

"It happened," Lisa stated. "I've never felt more ashamed in my life! I really have wonderful luck with men, don't I?" she asked ironically. "First Kevin, who wanted to have a relationship and yet be free to roam at the same time, and now a man who believes the worst of me and sets out to shame me! I'm through with men," she added shakily, "for the rest of my life."

Roni laughed outright. "Don't be silly. You're too pretty. The male population as a whole will never let you. Besides, just because there've been a couple of rotten apples in the barrel, you—"

She was interrupted by the telephone ringing. She leapt to her feet. "That might be Jack," she said hopefully.

But after she answered it, she covered the mouthpiece with her hand and turned toward Lisa. "For you," she mouthed.

"Tony?" Lisa's lips formed the word without making a sound.

Roni nodded.

Lisa shook her head and held up a hand. She would not talk to him. She couldn't. The pain quivering inside her was still too raw.

"I'm sorry," she heard Roni saying. Then there was silence and Roni, looking again at Lisa with a question in her eyes and receiving another negative signal, said, "I can't help it, Tony. She won't come to the phone. Yes, I'll tell her."

When she returned to the sofa, Roni's eyes were thoughtful. "He really sounded distraught, Lisa. Whatever he did, I think he's honestly sorry for it. Why don't you give him a break and call him back?"

"No." Lisa was adamant. "I don't want anything more to do with him. Not ever."

"How long have you known you were in love with him?"

Lisa stared at her roommate. "How did you know?" she asked at last.

Roni shrugged, then a pixieish grin peeked out from behind her sober expression. "I'm in love, too, remember? It's easy to read the signs. If you didn't love him, you'd at least listen to his apology because it really wouldn't matter that much one way or the other."

Lisa was spared the effort of having to respond to that when the telephone rang a second time. She tensed. "I still don't want to speak to him."

Roni shrugged. "Have it your way."

But when she picked up the receiver, her quick "How is he?" told Lisa the other party on the line was Jack, calling from San Diego. She got up and went into her bedroom so that Roni could talk without an audience.

By morning, Lisa was far from rested. She had tossed and turned half the night. She stumbled into the bathroom for a shower, but even that failed to make her feel much better.

When she went back to her bedroom to dress, she resisted the urge to crawl back into the bed. She had to catch a bus to Santa Barbara so that she could set about getting her car repaired. A long bus ride and a day hanging around a garage was daunting enough. The knowledge that she would probably have to see Tony when she went onto his property to retrieve her car was downright terrifying. She didn't know how she was going to manage to keep a lid on all the emotions that battled within her. She was still furious with him; but she was also sad. Her self-respect told her she shouldn't care about him anymore, but deep down she knew she did. It hurt to know her love had been so misplaced. Most of all, it hurt to know how little Tony truly thought of her, in spite of his attempt to call last night with some sort of apology.

Lisa slipped into jeans and a pullover shirt, then went to the kitchen. She put on the coffee and just then Roni came into the room, neatly dressed in a pair of dark slacks and a soft print blouse.

"How'd Jack say his brother was when he called last night?" Lisa asked as she put sausages into a frying pan.

"Not as seriously injured as they first thought, thank goodness. He's pretty banged up, but they say he'll make it."

"That's good news," Lisa said. "I know his family must be relieved."

"Yes, they are," Roni said. "So am I—" The jangling of the telephone cut off whatever else she had been about to say. She moved toward the door, saying over her shoulder, "That's probably Jack now."

Lisa was putting bread into the toaster a moment later when she came back. "It's Tony," she stated calmly, just as though she weren't dropping a bomb into the quiet morning routine.

Lisa caught her lower lip between her teeth. "Say I'm still asleep," she said quickly.

"I already admitted you're awake. Come on, Lisa," Roni said persuasively, "the guy is determined to talk to you, so you might as well give in to the inevitable."

Lisa shook her head and said stiffly, "I'm too busy." She reached into the cupboard for plates and, in her agitation, dropped one. It crashed to the floor and splintered into a thousand pieces. In frustration, she glared at Roni. "Now look what happened! The man makes me crazy! Tell him to stop calling, please!"

But if Roni told him that, he didn't pay any attention. Or at least Lisa assumed it was Tony calling again after Roni left for work. The phone rang three different times while she was cleaning the kitchen, writing out a couple of bills to put in the mail and making her bed. She ignored it and finally it rang no more.

At a little after nine, Lisa left the apartment. She would catch a city bus nearby that would take her to the station where she would board another bus. With any luck, by midafternoon she would have a tow truck hauling her car to the garage. However, if the mechanics couldn't get it repaired today, she'd have to take yet another bus home and repeat the whole process again next week. She was beginning to wonder if the car was worth all the trouble involved.

She locked the door and ran down the outside stairs toward the walkway. Because she was in a hurry, she didn't even lift her head as she went down the steps, so she was unprepared when her feet left the last step and she ran into a solid wall that shouldn't have been there.

Lisa gasped as two strong arms went around her waist, steadying her. She had a hazy impression of long, powerful male legs clad in tight-fitting jeans, a blue plaid western shirt with pearl buttons and a blue denim jacket before she looked up. When she did, shock waves rippled through her.

A slightly crooked grin spread across Tony's face as he gazed down at her. "Good morning." He said the words as casually as if they were no more than scarcely acquainted neighbors being polite in passing. His hands dropped away from her waist.

Lisa was in no mood to even pretend politeness. He'd humiliated her beyond forgiveness last night; she'd gone home to a miserable night of almost no sleep at all; obviously he thought that annoying her with a lot of phone calls and now a personal visit so that he could offer her a breezy little apology would set everything right, but he was dead wrong. She wasn't so easily placated and on top of everything else, if she didn't get moving, she was going to miss her bus.

"Go away," she snapped. She moved around him and strode down the walkway.

Tony was suddenly beside her, his tan boots easily keeping pace with her hurried footsteps. "It's a nice day, don't you think? Nice enough, even, for a swim in the stream."

Lisa glared at him. "Is that supposed to be funny?"

"Maybe not hilarious, but humorous at least."

"You don't see me laughing, do you?" They had reached the city sidewalk and Lisa swung to the left.

Tony stayed with her. "Where are we going in such a hurry?" he asked conversationally.

"I'm going to catch a bus so I can get my car." Abruptly Lisa stopped and held out her hand. "I'd appreciate it if you'd give me the key to the gate."

Tony cocked his head to one side, assessing her. "And if I don't?"

"Then I'll pick the damn lock!" she sputtered. She resumed walking.

He caught up with her again and heaved a loud sigh. "You're the most exasperating woman I've ever met! Can't you stop for one minute so I can apologize to you?"

"All right, you've apologized. Good-bye." Lisa kept going, never missing a step.

"I also came to offer you a ride to the ranch."

"I'll get there on my own," she replied ungraciously.

"Why are you being so obstinate?" he demanded. "You know taking the bus means a longer, less comfortable trip. Besides, it doesn't make any sense as long as I'm already going up there anyway. I'll be perfectly happy to give you a lift."

"I don't need any favors from you!" Lisa snapped.

"Tsk, tsk." Tony clucked his tongue. "You know, you're awfully cute when you get mad, but you're beautiful when you're amorous."

Outrage poured over her like boiling water. Lisa's arm shot up and only Tony's quick alertness stopped her hand from making violent contact with his face. His fingers closed around her wrist and for an endless moment they stood there on the sidewalk in broad daylight, with her arm stretched high and his hand imprisoning her there.

"Let go of me," she hissed beneath her breath. The measured tone of her voice was warning enough of just how furious she was.

Abruptly, Tony pivoted and, still gripping her wrist, pulled her around with him. His long legs moved rapidly along the sidewalk, back the way they had come, and Lisa was helpless to do anything other than stumble hurriedly along beside him.

"Let go of me!" By now she was trembling with fury.

"I think not," he said firmly. "We're wasting time and I'm anxious to get on the road."

"I am not going with you!" she exclaimed.

"Of course you are. Don't be silly," he chided.

Lisa twisted her arm, but his hold on her was unyielding. "If I scream, you're going to look ridiculous."

Tony shook his head and grinned. "No. You will."

"I hate you!" she said in a vibrating voice.

"I already know that," he said calmly. "Therefore, I figure I have nothing to lose."

"Except your freedom!" she retorted. "Which is what will happen when I have you arrested for kidnapping."

"We'll see," he said as though he were humoring her. He paused long enough to look down at her and add, "You know, we'd get along a lot better if you'd just cooperate a teensy bit. Now come along. We've still got to pack an overnight bag for you. Unless you want to borrow my robe and Maggie's clothes again."

Lisa dug in her heels and glared at him. "Are you stark, raving mad? There's no way I'm going up there and spend the night alone in that cabin with you!"

Tony grinned at her. "You have nothing to worry about," he told her. "You'll be adequately chaperoned and protected from my unwelcome advances. Maggie called early this morning to say she'd be there for the weekend."

"And you think *that* makes me feel better?" she demanded incredulously. "You definitely are mad if you think I'll stay there one minute with you and your girl friend!"

Tony continued to smile. "Oh, you'll like Maggie," he assured her. "Now, let's see about getting your clothes."

"I will not," she said stubbornly. "How many times do I have to say it? I'm not going with you and I'm not packing any bags!"

They were back in front of the apartment complex by then. "Fine," Tony said easily. "I'll pack it for you, then." Abruptly, he released her wrist and at the same time snatched her purse strap from her shoulder.

Taking long strides, he headed toward the stairs. Lisa stared after him. His arrogance was unbelievable! Pressing her lips together angrily, she ran after him.

When she reached the apartment, he'd already opened the door and gone straight to her bedroom. There she found him rummaging through her dresser drawers. He pulled out a pair of bikini panties. "Nice," he murmured as he tossed them on the bed. Next came a bra and he grinned at her wickedly. "That's nice, too, but will we need it? You don't always wear one, as I recall."

Lisa inhaled deeply and, when she knew she had control, asked with deceptive sweetness, "Aren't you the least bit concerned about being murdered in your bed tonight?"

Tony extracted a pair of shorts from another drawer, then moved toward the closet. "Hmmm, that might be a possibility," he conceded. He glanced at her and said, "Remind me to stop on the way and buy a lock for the bedroom door."

Lisa shook her head. "You're impossible! Tony, will you please stop going through my things? I am not going to spend the night at your cabin! Even if I wanted to, I couldn't. I have plans tonight with Roni.''

"And you told me you never lied!'' Tony scolded.

"What do you mean by that?''

He gave her a knowing grin. "I told Roni this morning that I planned to take you to the ranch for the entire weekend. She happened to mention that she'd be in San Diego with Jack's family.'' He found a small bag on the floor of her closet and, placing it on the bed, began stuffing her clothes into it.

In exasperation, Lisa threw up her hands. "All right, so I fibbed. Listen to me, Tony, and stop this craziness! Give me one good reason why I should go with you.''

Gripping the bag, he walked over to her and suddenly his face was devoid of all teasing. "Because I intend to keep apologizing to you about last night until you really accept it. Because you've repeatedly said we didn't really know each other and you're right. This weekend will be a good opportunity to get better acquainted. And most of all, because I want your company. So, is all that so terrible?''

He was standing so close that a kind of deadening inertia came over her. It always seemed to happen when he was so near. It slowed down her thinking processes, so that it was difficult to remain cool and possessed; it had a way of affecting her senses so that she didn't want to move away. There was a special magnetic quality about him that bound her where she was and made her bones turn to water and her body anticipate his touch.

But he didn't touch her now. "Is that so terrible?'' he repeated softly.

"I . . . don't know," she replied truthfully.

Tony's smile was gentle. "Then come spend the weekend and let's find out."

Lisa shook her head. "I don't think . . . there's Maggie and—" She broke off in a helpless tangle of confusion.

Tony took her hand. "I told you before not to worry about her. If you're thinking competition, you're wrong."

It was precisely what she was thinking, of course. "You said once she's your best girl," she reminded.

He grinned and a glint of teasing crept into his eyes. "That's right. She always has been and nothing will ever change that, not ever. But that doesn't mean there's not room in my life for another best girl."

Lisa flared at that. "You've got a hell of a nerve! You were furious at me when you thought I was spreading my affections around! I have no more intention of putting up with it from a man than you did from me and . . ."

Tony set the overnight bag on the floor, then placed both his hands to the wall on either side of her. He ended her objections by leaning forward and kissing her soundly.

When he released her at last, he said solemnly, "I wouldn't expect you to tolerate anything like that and I'm not asking you to. Just come with me, Lisa, and meet Maggie and see for yourself. If you don't like her and don't want to stay, I'll bring you home."

Lisa looked doubtful. "Promise?"

He nodded. "I promise." He picked up the bag once more, then took her arm with his free hand. "Let's go."

Lisa went, but she was far from reassured. As she got into the car with Tony, she couldn't help but wonder if she wasn't placing herself in the position of being made a complete fool of for the second day in a row. Just because Tony was behaving as though he cared about her meant nothing. Look what had happened last night! She felt vulnerable and uncertain and extremely uneasy about the whole situation. Who was this Maggie Tony spoke of so fondly? And how could Tony be so certain they would like each other? Why should he even want them to meet?

The questions whirled in her head as Tony drove out of the parking area onto the street, and when she glanced at his profile she found no answers. Nervously, and still half-angry that she'd been weak enough to allow him to talk her into going with him after all, Lisa hunched down in her seat.

From the corner of his eye, Tony saw the unhappy gesture. He sighed inwardly, knowing he had his work cut out to win back Lisa's trust in him. Not that he could blame her for being wary of his intent after the stunt he'd pulled last night! He'd been crazy with jealousy and pain, but that didn't excuse his abominable behavior. He was lucky that he'd gotten her to speak to him at all this morning and he was phenomenally fortunate that he'd been able to convince her to come with him. It had been touch and go there for a while and he could still hardly believe she was here in the car with him. It was a better break than he deserved and he knew it. Now the trick was going to be in getting her to relax and be comfortable with him again. If he blew it this weekend, he knew it would be over for good. She'd never have another thing to do with him. In the meantime, he was aware of the thickening silence between them, which was only going to get worse unless he did something about it and fast.

"My favorite foods are a thick broiled steak, shrimp fixed any way imaginable, potatoes in any form and banana pudding. What're yours?"

Lisa stared at him blankly. "I beg your pardon?" she asked politely.

Tony grinned. "I'm trying to get acquainted and I figured starting with the basics was a good move. What are your favorite foods?"

He was gratified to see that he had won a smile, albeit a reluctant, lukewarm one.

"Most anything, really," she answered. "I like ethnic dishes of any kind, especially Chinese and Mexican. And I'm a fanatic about homemade bread."

"Do you bake it yourself?"

Lisa nodded. "As often as I can. I especially enjoy the flavor of sourdough bread. I always keep the starter on hand."

"I hope you'll let me sample a loaf sometime."

She gave him a considering look. "We'll see," she said noncommittally.

The comment told him clearly she was still holding him at a distance. But at least, he thought ruefully, she hadn't said "no." He tried again. "The foods I hate are beets and brussels sprouts. Come to think of it, I also hate those alfalfa sprouts some people sprinkle on salads. Alfalfa's for cattle, not people," he said indignantly.

This time Lisa laughed out loud and the sound of it warmed something in Tony that had been iced over for the past two weeks. He gripped the steering wheel with both hands to restrain the urge to reach over and touch her. It was too soon. He'd gotten away with that kiss back in her apartment, but he wasn't a man who believed in pushing his luck.

"Alfalfa's supposed to be very good for your health," she told him in a prim, schoolteacherish manner.

"So are some pretty nasty-tasting medicines, but I don't inflict them on myself unless I'm sick!"

Lisa giggled and Tony was glad to see she looked far less tense than she had a few minutes earlier.

"When I was little, my parents used to bribe me to take my medicine by letting me crawl in between them to sleep. I can remember how cuddly and warm that felt and then Daddy would tell me a story." She smiled reminiscently. "He was a champion story-teller. He could make up some real whoppers! Mom used to complain that he did it all wrong. Instead of making me sleepy, he'd get me so interested and excited I'd beg for more."

"That sounds like heaven," Tony said gruffly.

Lisa looked at him sharply and said contritely, "I'm sorry. I should have remembered—"

Tony cut her off. "About my dreary childhood?" He shook his head. "Don't worry. You didn't hurt my feelings. To tell the truth, I like hearing stories like that about normal families. Your parents," he added with a smile, "sound like wonderful people."

"They are." Lisa's voice was husky.

"Tell me about them," he encouraged.

"Well, Dad's a retired geologist and Mom's your typical housewife. They live in Arizona now and love it.

Dad plays golf and Mom does volunteer work at a hospital, belongs to a bridge club and watches Dad's health like a hawk. He had a heart attack three years ago that frightened us pretty badly, but he seems to be doing fine now." She paused for a moment, then asked, "What about you? Those things I read . . . were they true?"

Tony's jaw hardened unconsciously and he nodded. "Afraid so. My father abandoned us when I was very young. I was ten when my mother decided she was tired of being a mother and walked out on me."

"It must have been . . . horrible!"

Tony heard the catch in her voice. "Don't go wasting any pity on me," he told her quickly. "Actually, it was the best thing that ever happened to me, even though I didn't know it at the time, of course. Lisa, you read those articles. They even pointed out that before I was ten I was taken to juvenile court a couple of times for shoplifting. What the reporter didn't know was that my mother was the one who put me up to it."

Lisa gasped in horror and her eyes suddenly filled with tears. "Tony," she said softly, "how awful for you!"

"Yes." His voice was grim. "It was. I can still remember how scared I was, thinking I was going to jail!" He gave a shrug, as though trying to throw off those old emotions. "Anyway," he said in a more normal voice a moment later, "after she dumped me and took off with her boyfriend, I was sent to a series of foster homes. Some of them weren't so bad, but others were miserable. Even so, no matter how dreadful they seemed, I got three square meals a day, a bed to sleep in and nobody forced me to do anything like stealing."

"I . . . I can scarcely even comprehend such a child-hood, my own was so different," Lisa said in a low voice. "I was always so secure, so loved." She looked over at Tony's strained face. "That's the reason you made that donation to the foundation, isn't it? Because of how terrible things were for you?"

Tony nodded. "I was one of the lucky kids who got out of that kind of life. Because I finally met a couple who cared enough to take me in and turn my life around. I made it big, first as an athlete, then as a businessman, but I could never have done it if they hadn't given me a chance. They encouraged me, made me see my potential, made me believe in myself and my abilities and were absolutely loving tyrants when it came to the importance of educa-tion. How can I possibly turn my back on other kids who are like I was? I know a camp won't solve their day-to-day problems. A lot of them will never have much of a chance at life, no matter what somebody like me does. But if just a handful of kids ever benefit from kind words, encour-agement and the vocational skills they can pick up at the camp that might help them later when they're on their own, then it'll be worth it."

"I think it's wonderful of you," Lisa said quietly.

She was amazed at his explosive outburst. "Wonderful, hell!" Tony practically snarled at her. "Don't go making me out to be noble, because I'm not! It's simply some-thing I had to do, like breathing, and I see no good reason for what I did to ever be published for everybody to read about!"

"I already told you I wouldn't write about it," Lisa said calmly.

Tony gave her a sheepish smile that made her heart do a flip. "I forgot," he said in an ordinary tone of voice. "Sorry. I guess I'm just on edge because I'm not used to talking about myself like this."

Something in his manner warned Lisa that he didn't want to discuss the subject any further. She'd been able to tell by the strain in Tony's voice that talking about the past was a painful experience for him, and because of it she'd realized even before he told her that she was being singled out for such a confidence. Why was he doing it? To win back her trust in him by first trusting her?

But she couldn't quite do that. She felt a great deal of compassion for the child Tony, and all he had endured. No matter how much he objected, she also admired the adult Tony who gave so generously to other unfortunate children. She even appreciated his openness with her just now. But none of that altered what had occurred between them. He had hurt her badly last night and while she might be able to forgive him, she wasn't so sure she could ever put her faith in him again.

Even with all her doubts, Lisa's heart went right on quietly insisting that Tony was the only man she would ever love. If things didn't work out, if he didn't return that love, how would she ever make it through all the years ahead? She'd known him only a short while, but already the thought of a lifetime without him loomed like a journey with no aim, no purpose, no direction. Yet she had no choice but to face up to that almost certain probability.

In Santa Barbara Tony stopped at a garage, and by the time they were on their way again, it was with the assurance that within an hour a tow truck would be sent for Lisa's car.

It was nearly noon when they passed between the gateposts at the ranch. Besides Lisa's car, which was still where she'd left it near the front gate, there was a small green Datsun parked near the cabin. The sight of it forcibly reminded Lisa of Tony's other guest and her own reluctance to meet his adored Maggie.

Apparently sensing her dread, Tony gave her an encouraging smile when he parked his car beside the smaller one. "I hope Maggie's fixed something good to eat for lunch," he said. "I'm starving."

Lisa, on the other hand, felt as though she could never eat another bite. It had been a mistake to ride up here with Tony today. He'd been so friendly that he had seriously undermined her defenses against him. It would also be a mistake to meet the woman in the cabin who was waiting for him. That was suddenly, blindingly clear. If she did, she would only be hurt again, despite Tony's assurances otherwise.

"I've decided," she said firmly. "I'm not going inside."

Tony looked at her incredulously. "What're you talking about?"

"You said I didn't have to stay if I didn't want to. Well, I don't want to. I'll just wait in my car for the tow truck and ride back to town with the driver. You won't need to bother with me anymore."

"Forget it!" Tony was adamant. "You promised you'd meet Maggie and *then* decide if you wanted to leave. I'm holding you to our bargain."

Lisa could be equally stubborn. She set her jaw in a hard line. "I'm not going in there and let you humiliate me another time!"

"You are going in, even if I have to sling you across my shoulders and carry you! As for humiliation, you're only going to end up doing that to yourself if you hang about outside like a timid little mouse!" He rolled his eyes upward. "Lord, give me the patience to deal with such an obstinate woman!" Then, like a cat pouncing upon the mouse he'd just called her, he snatched her into his arms and smothered her face with kisses.

The passionate assault went on for several minutes and every time Lisa tried to squirm away, he only held her tighter. The kisses went on without end . . . her lips, her cheeks, her eyes, her forehead, even her throat and earlobes. It was as though her refusal to go inside had released a flood of pent-up emotions and he didn't intend to let her go until they were all spent.

But then a feminine voice interrupted, calling from a distance, "Tony, aren't you going to come inside?"

When Tony drew back, his breath fanned Lisa's cheeks like fire and his eyes were glassy and unfocused. Both of them were trembling.

"Damn!" he exclaimed under his breath. "Maggie's timing is atrocious! I guess we'd better go join her."

Pale and unsteady, Lisa let Tony help her out of the car. Nervously, she turned toward the cabin and the woman who was so important in Tony's life.

Chapter Nine

The woman coming down the porch steps was everything Lisa had imagined, except for one thing. About Lisa's own height, she was slender as a teenager and her denim jeans enhanced her long, shapely legs. She wore a plaid shirt, open at the throat, and western boots on her feet. Her shoulder-length blond hair bounced as she ran forward and a lively sparkle danced in her blue eyes. Her golden skin bespoke a love for the outdoors and there were even a few appealing freckles sprinkled across her nose. She was also at least fifteen years older than Tony, a fact that totally confounded Lisa.

"Darling!" she exclaimed as she opened her arms and rushed toward Tony. "It's so good to see you!"

Tony wrapped his arms around her, lifted her off her

feet and swung her around. "You look terrific, Maggie, my love," he said, laughing as he held her aloft.

Maggie beat her fists playfully against his broad shoulders. "Let me down this minute, you big gorilla! Behave yourself!"

Lisa felt acutely uncomfortable as she watched the exuberant greeting. Tony had called Maggie "my love" and it was obvious that while she was calling him less flattering names, she, in turn, was extremely fond of him. Lisa had never felt more in the way in all her life. She had dreaded this moment all morning and now it was worse than she had expected. She swallowed painfully over the knot in her throat and lowered her gaze to the ground.

"Put me down!" Maggie ordered again. "You're being rude, Tony! You haven't introduced me to your friend."

Reluctantly, Lisa lifted her head and saw that this time Tony had obeyed. The other woman was now on her feet, though Tony's arm went around her waist as the two of them walked together toward her.

"Hi, I'm Maggie Borden," she said, extending her hand. Her smile was engaging and warm. Her blue eyes were robin's-egg soft and laugh lines crinkled around the edges. "I apologize for that little clown act, but sometimes Tony's apt to forget both his manners and the fact that he's supposed to be a dignified adult. He just reverts to being an impish boy again."

Tony chuckled. "You keep me feeling young, Maggie, you're so young yourself. Let me introduce you to Lisa Knight."

"I'm delighted to meet you, Lisa," Maggie said, sounding as though she really meant it.

In spite of herself, Lisa found that she couldn't help liking the older woman. She smiled and said a little shyly, "I'm pleased to meet you, too."

"Come inside," Maggie said to them both. "I've got lunch ready."

"What did you fix for me?" Tony asked eagerly, sounding to Lisa for all the world exactly like what Maggie had just called him—a little boy.

"Chicken and dumplings," Maggie answered as she led the way up the porch steps.

"Ah, you're spoiling me again," Tony said with a satisfied smile. "I can taste it already."

Maggie paused on the porch to give him a fond pat on his cheek. "Well, I don't get the opportunity to do that very often for either one of my boys these days." She glanced at Lisa, as though not to exclude her and, at the surprised expression on her face, exclaimed, "Hasn't Tony explained our relationship to you?"

Lisa shook her head and felt her face redden. "Not . . . not really."

Maggie looked suddenly suspicious. She placed a hand on her hip and tapped her little finger against a pocket as she demanded, "Just what did he tell you about me?"

"Nothing really. Except that you were his best girl and he adores you," Lisa said bluntly.

Maggie turned on Tony and shook a finger in his face. "Anthony Paul Neugent," she said sternly, "if you weren't bigger than I am, I'd give you the spanking you deserve for putting the wrong idea into this poor girl's head!"

Far from looking contrite, Tony threw back his head

and laughed heartily. "Well, it's the truth, isn't it?" he asked. "I do adore you and you know you've always been my best girl."

"I'll deal with you later," Maggie said in a tart voice. She turned back to Lisa. "My dear, since I raised this big lug from the time he was fourteen, I can only apologize for his boorish lack of good manners. I thought I had taught him better."

Lisa stared at her. "You mean you're . . ."

Maggie smiled. "I'm his foster mother."

Tony draped an arm across her shoulders and smiled down at her with open affection. "This lady," he told Lisa with a slight catch in his voice, "taught me what it means to belong to a family. She took a sullen, scared kid with a lot of false bravado and no future and turned him into a confident man with an education and a set of values. Can you blame me for loving her to distraction?"

"Hey, lighten up!" Maggie poked Tony in the ribs. "You're embarrassing me. Besides, I had a lot of good raw material to work with. Even so"—her tone became stern again—"your saying nice things about me isn't going to get you off the hook so easily. It was terrible of you to let Lisa think I was your girl friend! I'm surprised," she said to Lisa, "that you even came up here with him today if you thought that."

Lisa grinned. "He threatened to kidnap me if I didn't come willingly."

Maggie stared balefully at Tony and shook her head. "Son, son, what's come over you? And once you were such a nice boy!"

"Lisa was coming anyway to see about her car"—Tony

waved a hand toward the main gate—"but I had to do something a little drastic to get her to ride up with me instead of taking the bus."

"Aha, a lover's tiff," Maggie said wisely. "I knew it. That's why you let her think I was a girl friend. Really, Tony, that sort of thing could backfire."

He grinned. "It almost did. Even though I finally more or less told her you weren't, I had a helluva time convincing her to spend the weekend with us."

"I should think so!" Maggie took Lisa's hand. "Come on inside for lunch and I'll leave it to your discretion as to whether Tony should get any or not."

"What?" Tony sounded outraged as he followed them through the door. "You wouldn't, couldn't be so cruel as to deny me chicken and dumplings."

"That's entirely up to Lisa," Maggie stated firmly. "You certainly deserve some sort of punishment."

"Lisa?" Tony asked in a pleading voice. He gave her a pitiful look, like that of a poor, starving puppy.

She laughed at him, suddenly feeling exhilarated, and she pretended to give the matter some thought. "You can have your lunch," she said finally, "only if you give me your firm promise never to tease me like that again."

"I promise." His dark eyes, warm and clear, met hers and his lips parted in a soft smile. As Maggie went on toward the kitchen, he whispered, "Now am I forgiven?"

Lisa shook her head. "Not by a long shot." But the words lacked conviction because she couldn't help smiling back. After the dark despair of the night before, such swift, pure happiness was as welcome as a gust of breeze on a hot summer day.

Over lunch, Tony asked Maggie, "How was your cruise?"

"Very nice. We met some lovely people on board. Oh, and I'm quite proud of myself." Maggie laughed. "I didn't get seasick even once."

"Good for you. Why didn't you come out to the Malibu house when you got back to port?"

Maggie wrinkled her nose. "To tell you the truth, I needed a quiet rest. I love my friend Ruth, but honestly, after a week of her nonstop chatter, I just wanted to be alone for a few days before I go on to San Francisco to visit Amy. I really didn't plan to see her this trip, but when she found out I'd be in California, she insisted."

"You wanted to be alone, hmmm?" Tony asked with deceptive blandness. "By the way, how is Jim?"

Maggie suddenly looked self-conscious. "Now, Tony, don't start!"

Tony winked at Lisa. "Jim Whitney is a widower who owns a ranch about five miles down the road. For the past two years, he's burned up that road every time Maggie's come to visit. He even asked my permission to marry her, but she just keeps him dangling, poor man!"

"I don't think he's suffering too much," Maggie said. "I heard rumors in Solvang that no less than three women are chasing him. If that's true, I doubt he's been sitting around brooding much over me."

"So what time are we expecting him for dinner tonight?" Tony asked, cutting through her smokescreen.

"Seven," Maggie replied.

Tony met Lisa's amused gaze and winked again.

Maggie saw it and gave a reluctant grin, although her eyes dared him to say another word on the subject.

While they ate, Lisa learned that Maggie had a nineteen-year-old son named Bill who had just completed his first year of college in New York State and who was working this summer for a construction company. Although their home had been in Chicago, after Bill's graduation from high school last year Maggie had sold her home and bought another one near her married sister in North Carolina, where she'd been born and raised.

"It just didn't feel like home anymore after my husband Cal died five years ago," she explained to Lisa. "But I hung on and stayed while Bill was still in school because it would have been just that much harder if I'd uprooted him on top of losing his father."

"Wasn't it hard, though?" Lisa asked. "My parents sold their home in Oklahoma after Dad retired and moved to Arizona. While they love it now, it took them a while to adjust. For the first few months, they thought they'd made a mistake."

"I felt that way, too," Maggie admitted. "It was hard to leave the house Cal and I had bought together as newlyweds and where we raised two rambunctious boys, but there comes a time when you just have to let go and make a new start. With Cal gone, Tony out here and Bill off in New York, there was nothing to keep me there anymore, although I have gone back once to visit friends. But overall, I'm content living near my sister. When all's said and done, family is what really counts." She smiled. "That's enough about me. Tell me about yourself, Lisa. What do you do for a living?"

"You're not going to believe this," Tony said before Lisa could speak, "but she's a journalist."

Maggie's eyes widened and she looked genuinely startled. "No joking? You're actually on speaking terms with a reporter?"

"Off and on," Tony admitted with a little laugh. "But it's been rocky." He gave Lisa a warm smile that was calculated to melt a glacier.

Maggie shook her head. "I can't believe it. What sort of things do you write?" she asked Lisa. "Obviously nothing about Tony."

"And live to tell about it, you mean?" Lisa laughed. "Of course I wanted to write about him and I never received so much abuse from a potential subject in my life. It's almost been bad enough to make me reconsider my career choice."

"But are you?" Maggie asked. "Going to write about him, I mean?"

Lisa shook her head. "No," she said quietly. "Not now. I gave him my word that I wouldn't."

"Although she tempts me," Tony said. "If I ever did decide to grant another interview, Lisa would get it."

His eyes met hers and the tenderness in his gaze made Lisa's heart flutter. Once again, she was falling under his magical spell, being drawn to him by an irresistible force that was stronger than logic. The painful episode of the night before was submerged beneath new layers of unbridled hope. Because she loved him, she was a hapless victim, deeply affected by Tony's every mood. If he was angry, she was in despair; if he was hurt, she felt his pain; if he was teasing, she became giddy and lighthearted; and when he became gentle and looked at her with such intimate affection that the rest of the world seemed to fade away, her heart responded as truly and naturally as season follows season. He was the answer to all the hopes and dreams she'd ever had, the other half of her completeness. He had stormed her emotions, plundered her heart and insinuated himself so strongly into her mind that nothing else seemed to have meaning without him.

By five, Lisa's car was ready. Before they drove into town to get it, while Lisa took a shower, Tony put charcoal in the grill and started the fire. The coals would burn down while they were gone and be ready, by the time they returned, for the thick steaks he had taken from the freezer.

The three of them had spent a pleasant afternoon checking on a cow and her calf, putting out supplemental feed for the cattle, and later, while Tony had chopped wood for the fireplace, Lisa and Maggie had taken turns mowing the grass around the cabin.

Tony couldn't remember the last time he'd ever felt so happy and content. The two women he cared most about in all the world had quickly taken to each other and that pleased him immensely. Deep inside, there had been a small, nagging anxiety because he'd wanted it so much. Nothing and no one could ever change the way he felt about Maggie or the enormous debt he felt he owed her. He knew he would never be able to pay her back for all she and Cal had done for him, even if he lived a thousand years, but it would have bothered him greatly if she had disapproved of Lisa, or if Lisa had disliked her.

He didn't try to kid himself any longer. He was in love with Lisa, deeply, irrevocably in love with her. How it had happened in such a short time he had no idea, but here it was. He'd really known it the night they'd made love. Only caution, a reluctance to open himself up to another human being, had kept him from trusting his feelings. He'd once thought he was in love with Carmen and look how that had turned out. Not that what he felt for Lisa bore any resemblance to what he'd felt for Carmen. This was different, rooted right down to his soul, whereas the other had been superficial. But in his experience, women he cared about only betrayed and hurt him. His own mother had been the most treacherous of all. In all the years since she'd deserted him, he'd never been able to love any woman without some reservations except for Maggie, and that was far different from the kind of love a man feels for a woman on an intimate plane.

But he was unsure of exactly how Lisa felt about him. He knew she cared, but how much? Last night he had done great damage to whatever feelings she did have for him and though she had gradually thawed toward him throughout the day, he had a gut instinct that it was going to take a Herculean effort on his part to pierce through her defensive armor.

It helped, though, having Maggie there. Her presence seemed to relax Lisa, making her less guarded than she might otherwise have been. Tony determined to take things slow and easy and try to rebuild gradually what one insane moment on his part had destroyed. As long as he kept things light, Lisa seemed fine, but he noticed that every time he looked at her with his feelings plain to see, she became fidgety and nervous.

They went for the car and during the drive Tony kept his resolve to maintain a casual, impersonal demeanor. When Lisa told him she'd never been to the Santa Barbara Mission, he promised to take her there one day when there was time. "A candle's been kept burning on the altar since 1786," he told her.

"I remember reading something about that," Lisa said. "I would like to see it sometime."

"You will," he stated with quiet emphasis. "If you're really interested in missions, there's another one just outside of Solvang. It's been restored and has a lot of interesting religious artifacts."

"Isn't Solvang where they have the Danish festival?"

Tony nodded. "And where they have a lot of Danish bakeries. Maybe we'll drive over tomorrow morning and buy some pastries for breakfast. They're out of this world!"

When they got back to the ranch, Jim Whitney was already there, occupying a lawn chair near the grill and sipping a beer.

"Hope you don't mind, Tony, but I went ahead and put the steaks on to cook. Maggie asked me to because after we eat, we're going into Santa Barbara to play bridge with some friends of mine."

"Fine," Tony replied. He introduced Jim to Lisa and then Maggie came out of the house carrying a tablecloth and plates for the picnic table.

Jim Whitney was a large, likable man with a good sense of humor and an easy flow of talk. He found as much to say to Lisa as he did to Tony or Maggie and Lisa couldn't help but feel at ease in his company.

After dinner Lisa insisted on doing the dishes without Maggie's help so she and Jim could leave. After a certain amount of good-natured arguing, Maggie gave in and the older couple drove away.

Tony helped Lisa with the cleaning up and though he kept the conversation on strictly neutral ground and scarcely even looked her way, an odd little tension came over her. She was acutely sensitive to the fact that she was now alone here with him. She no longer trusted him to keep his distance from her; moreover, she didn't trust her own responses if he did make an advance.

When the kitchen was spotless, Tony said abruptly, "Let's go for a walk."

The sharp tone of his voice had something akin to anger in it. Lisa's eyes scanned his face, searching for the cause behind it. His features seemed strained, even a little colorless, as though he were keeping rigid control over his emotions.

Lisa was baffled by the sudden, inexplicable anger and she almost questioned him, but then she thought better of it. Everything between them was perplexing, unsettling and exhausting enough as it was.

Pretending she had noticed nothing different, she nodded and hung the dish towel on its rack. "Love to," she said without any particular inflection to her voice. "I need some exercise after that thick steak."

It was still light outside. Although the evening air was cool here among the hills, one could still detect a hint of summertime just around the corner. A gentle stillness lay upon the countryside as soft shadows fell. In the distance, the mountain peaks etched dark, jagged silhouettes against the sky. There was a timeless beauty about it all, the awesome grace and grandeur that only nature can provide.

For a long time, neither of them spoke. The only sound was that made by their own footsteps, and yet their silence was not an awkward one. The strange emotion that had come over Tony back in the kitchen seemed to have evaporated once they were outdoors and the quiet between them seemed only a natural extension of their peaceful surroundings, rather than a void that either should feel compelled to hastily fill.

They walked as far as the end of one pasture's fence line, probably a good half mile, before the silence was broken. By now dusk had cast a charcoal-gray blanket over the earth.

"It'll be dark soon," Tony said, squinting up at the sky, "and there's only a quarter-moon tonight. We'd better start back while we can still see where we're going."

Lisa turned readily and they strolled back the way they had come over the uneven ground.

"I like Maggie," she said, at last feeling the need to say something. She felt, rather than saw, Tony's smile.

"I know. She likes you, too."

"Why didn't you just tell me who she was instead of making such a mystery about her?"

"Exactly for the reason you think," he answered bluntly. "I wanted to make you as jealous as I've been. Did I succeed?"

Lisa held up a hand, as though to ward off the subject. "Tony, I'd really rather not discuss—"

He grabbed the hand and clasped it tightly. "I know, I know." His voice became impassioned and urgent. "I really blew it last night. All day long I've been trying to skirt around what really happened by teasing you and keeping things light, but that doesn't erase the damning truth. What I did was inexcusable, Lisa, I realize that." He released her hand and rubbed his forehead. "I went slightly berserk thinking about you and that man together, believing that while I was falling for you, you were playing fast and loose. You were right when you said I have a bad tendency to jump to conclusions, wrong conclusions, at that, but nothing is going to alter what I did. All I can do is beg your forgiveness and ask for a second chance."

A second chance. . . . Yet a chance for what? Lisa regarded him somberly in the waning light. Tony sounded sincere enough in his apology; he even looked abject, not at all like the tease he'd been this morning. But how could she be sure of him? Maybe he really did care for her, even as much as she did for him, but that didn't rule out the possibility of something similar happening again the very next time he got angry.

"I believe you're really sorry, Tony," she said, "and I accept your apology. But . . ."

"But?" he asked so softly it was scarcely more than his breath on the still evening air.

Lisa turned and began to walk again while she searched for the right words. "How do I know there won't someday be another outburst like last night? I . . . I honestly don't think I can deal with any more scenes like that one.''

"I know," he said humbly. "Normally, I'm not a violent-tempered man, Lisa, although I can see where you might have trouble believing that after what I did. I went off the deep end, wanting you so much and hating myself for wanting you, hating you because of what I thought you were doing. It had been festering inside me ever since that night I took you home and he was there waiting for you; and when you showed up last night, it just exploded. I'm not trying to excuse it, just explain it. Can you understand what I'm saying?"

Lisa mustered a tiny smile. "Actually, in a bizarre sort of way, you make sense."

Tony sighed heavily and grinned. "Then we're making a little progress." He pulled her into his arms and his embrace was warm and tender. "I've missed you," he whispered against her cheek. "You have no idea how much I've missed you."

Tears smarted in Lisa's eyes as she withdrew a little to look up into his face. She saw only sincerity in the dark glow of his eyes, in the somber set of his lips. "I've missed you, too, Tony," she said unsteadily. "Even so, I don't think I'm ready to . . . well, to . . ."

"To commit yourself again?"

She nodded.

He ran his hands up and down her arms. "I can understand that, even if I don't like it," he said huskily. "I want to make love to you, Lisa. Make no mistake about that. But I'll let you decide when. We've got all the time in the world, and when it happens I want it to be because you feel confident enough in me to know I won't hurt you like that ever again. I don't want you to have any doubts or fears." He pulled her close again and gave a crooked smile. "I can't promise not to touch you at all, though. My self-control does have its limits, especially when you stand there looking so beautiful and your lips are so soft and inviting!"

He kissed her with tenderness, yet it also bespoke an underlying urgency. His hand gently cradled her head and his mouth on hers was warm and persuasive, forceful with rising passion, but lacking any hint of dominance. Lisa sensed that he meant what he said and was holding himself back with tight restraint. It seemed as though Tony were afraid that if he revealed the true extent of his desire, she might skitter away like a frightened wild animal.

His kiss held the quality of a promise and Lisa felt much of the rigidity within herself draining away beneath the touching fragility of Tony's caress. Still, ambivalence held sway in her mind. Physically, she felt herself responding to the sweet pressure of his warm lips moving so softly on hers, yet a seed of doubt remained. If she were to give him the slightest indication of weakening, of yielding, she knew that the nature of his touch would change with lightning speed.

But she couldn't do it. Fear held her aloof, so that while she did not repulse him, neither could she invite anything more. She wasn't ready to lay herself wide open to that sort of pain again.

She saw that he realized that when they looked at each other again. Tony released her immediately and said prosaically, "We'd better go back."

Ridiculous disappointment swept over her, disappointment that his warm hands were no longer stroking her, that his lips were no longer pressed to hers, that the spreading heat in her body merely left her feeling shaky and dissatisfied. As they returned to the cabin, Lisa was disgusted with her conflicting reactions. She was no longer sure what it was she did want. If Tony touched her, she got nervous; when he didn't, she felt unhappy. Such opposing emotions were not in the least conducive to a restful mind and she felt edgy and tense.

Tony seemed to be no more at ease than she was. He made coffee, which they drank on the porch while they watched the stars begin to dust the sky, and though they carried on a conversation about a variety of impersonal subjects, Lisa knew they were both playing a game, tiptoeing around what was really uppermost in their thoughts. When . . . and how did they go from here? she wondered. Tony had said it would be up to her, but would she ever be able to make that first move?

She honestly didn't know, and the uncertainty grew as a strained and uneasy silence fell over them. For the past hour they had both tried, really tried, to pretend that the unanswered question didn't exist. They had talked about anything they could think of to pass the long minutes, but the truth was they were too acutely aware of each other physically to behave any longer as casual acquaintances. They'd gone far beyond that the first evening she'd been to the Malibu house and there was no going back now to a less involved relationship. She knew it; he knew it; yet there was still the wedge of last night between them.

The emotional struggle was suddenly overwhelming. Lisa's nerves were as taut as the barbed-wire fences. She stood up and said, "I'm really tired, Tony. If you don't mind, I think I'll go to bed."

He stood up, too, and his expression was concealed by the darkness that enveloped them. "Of course," he said politely. "You can have my room since Maggie's using the other bedroom."

"What about you?" she asked a little hesitantly.

"Damn it!" Tony erupted into anger. "I'm not going to try to sneak into the bed and force myself on you, if that's what's making you so nervous! Even I'm not that rotten!" He turned his back to her and, bracing his hands on the porch rail, gazed off into the night.

"I didn't mean to imply—" Lisa began stiffly.

Tony's harsh voice interrupted her words, although he kept his back to her. "I'll bunk on the sofa and I swear you'll be perfectly safe from me. Now, just go, will you?"

She wavered, her own pain recognizing his. The strain between them was fast widening into an unbridgeable chasm. Lisa wondered whether to go to him, wanting to; yet uncertainty held her back.

"Tony?" she ventured, almost whispering.

His voice was still gruff when he spoke again, but at least he no longer sounded so angry. "I'm sorry. I shouldn't have blown up like that. It's just so hard to be near you and know that . . ." He cleared his throat. "Forget it. Good night, Lisa."

"Are you . . . are you going to be all right?"

"Sure, sure. Good night," he said again, with such finality that it chilled her.

Tony's unmoving, tense stance was daunting and at last, not knowing what else to do, Lisa went inside and softly closed the door. When it clicked shut, it seemed to her to symbolize a permanence that tore at her heartstrings.

Chapter Ten

When the door closed, Tony's shoulders slumped and his mouth twisted in derision. All his life he'd been self-contained, always concealing his innermost feelings from others. A cool, remote demeanor had protected him from the world and even Maggie and Cal, who had known him better than anyone else and whom he had loved without qualification, had never completely penetrated his defenses. The deep core of him had remained his alone, inviolate, well hidden from the prying eyes of others. That part of him stood apart, neither needing nor wanting anyone else. It was his very essence, his life, the reality of his being, and he'd always felt somehow that to share it with another would mean the end of that which was uniquely himself. Yet now that Lisa had come into his life, he seemed a stranger to himself. One minute he was laying his heart on the line, openly showing her in every way he knew just how much he cared, even at the risk of total rejection, and the next he was a stick of dynamite blowing sky-high without warning, even to himself. No wonder Lisa was half afraid of him! With his emotions so volatile and supercharged, she must think he was a mental case in need of a psychiatrist's couch!

The whole thing seemed hopeless, anyway. His feelings for her were too intense, while Lisa, on the other hand, was so wary of him now that she hadn't even responded the slightest bit when he'd kissed her. It was entirely probable that his temporary insanity last night had killed whatever feeling she'd had for him. The trouble was that ever since they'd met, his reactions toward her had been ambivalent. Either he ached for her with a physical and mental hunger that was sheer torture or he was consumed by an equally passionate anger. The one thing he had never felt for her was indifference.

Tony had never loved anything or anyone with such fervor and the truth was such heated emotions frightened him. He found himself wanting to share everything with Lisa, thoughts and feelings he'd never before expressed, things he could buy for her, like a horse of her own or that trip to Europe she'd told him tonight she hoped someday to be able to take; he wanted her in his life, day and night, foul weather or fair, through all the ups and downs that would touch either of them for all time. Such desires were so alien to the philosophy of self-sufficiency he'd evolved through the years that he had to seriously question their validity.

He went down the steps and stood underneath the

canopy of stars. He inhaled several deep breaths and tried not to think about Lisa getting ready to sleep, alone, in his bed.

Lisa slipped into the white lacy nightgown Tony had packed for her and stood before the mirror to brush her hair. The gown fell in soft folds across the peaks of her breasts, down to skim her hips and on to swirl around her legs and ankles. Expertly cut, it lent an aura of ripe sensuality coupled with delicate feminity. It was not the sort of nightwear a woman normally chose for sleeping alone, and in fact, she had never worn it before. It had been a gift from Roni on her last birthday and Lisa had tucked it away in a bureau drawer for a vague "someday."

Seeing the unaccustomed image of herself in the mirror brought an ache to her throat, an ache that soon spread throughout her body. Abruptly, Lisa turned toward the huge bed beneath the window. Tony's bed. She swallowed painfully as she tried to visualize herself huddled alone beneath its covers.

The picture was unappealing and distressing, and in that instant all her uncertainty vanished and she knew what she had to do. Tony had apologized in every way he knew how today for his actions last night and beyond that, there was nothing else he could do. The rest was entirely up to her. He wasn't pushing, yet he made it abundantly evident that he still wanted her. She either believed he was sincere or she didn't; she either took a chance again or she didn't. It was as simple as that and now she knew that she would take that chance. If he hurt her again, so be it, but she had to find out. She would have no peace of mind until she knew, and what was a delay going to do to either of them except frustrate and even alienate them?

She smoothed her hair with trembling fingers, drew a long breath to steady her nerves and then, with determination propelling her, went toward the door.

When she opened it, she stopped abruptly and her heart thudded. Tony stood there, his hand upraised, about to knock. His arm lowered to his side and for a long while they gazed wordlessly at each other.

Tony swallowed and his voice was thick when he said at last, "You're unbelievably beautiful."

His words caused Lisa to realize that the lamplight in the room behind her must be silhouetting her body beneath the thin gown. His riveting gaze made her catch her breath, and though she felt a sudden shyness, she made no attempt to conceal herself.

Her throat felt dry when she tried to speak. "Tony, I was coming to . . ."

"Shhh," he whispered. Bridging the gap between them, he placed his forefinger to her lips. "Let me say what I came to say, please." He paused briefly, then went on in a rush. "I love you, Lisa. It's a very difficult thing for me to say because until I met you, I never did really believe in it. Maybe now's not the best time for me to tell you because I don't quite see how you can even believe it after the way I behaved, but I had to tell you before I lost my nerve. I'm . . . I'm not trying to pressure you about . . . anything. I just wanted you to know, that's all."

Lisa's eyes were soft and eloquent as she met his gaze. Tony's face was colorless while his dark eyes were so bright they almost appeared feverish. He looked absolutely shattered, as though he expected to be repulsed after his confession. For the first time she realized the true extent of his sensitivity. Earlier she'd known he was suffering pain just as she was, but even then she hadn't grasped the depths of it. Now she was being given a privileged glimpse right into a man's soul; he was openly exposing it for her view and he was vulnerable concerning what she might do with such power.

A great tenderness welled up inside of her and all she could think of was wiping away that fear of rejection from his eyes. Nothing else mattered, not the past, not the future, not even her own insecurities. She caught his trembling finger at her lips and kissed it lightly. "Tony," she murmured, half laughing, half crying, "I love you, too."

He went very still. "Don't say it if you don't really mean it," he said gruffly. "I couldn't stand it!" He seemed to be having difficulty speaking. "God knows I deserve the worst form of punishment, but please, don't play with me and say it if you don't mean it!"

Lisa curled her arms around his neck and, standing on tiptoe, brushed his lips with hers. "I love you," she repeated firmly. "That's why I was coming to find you, to tell you I don't want to sleep alone in your bed tonight."

"Lisa!" Tony's arms went around her waist and he crushed her to the solid breadth of his chest. His voice throbbed. "Darling, darling, are you sure?"

"I'm sure," she answered softly, just before his lips found hers.

Long minutes later, trembling and breathing raggedly, they turned, hand in hand, toward the inviting bed. Tony quickly stripped away his clothes and then helped Lisa out of her gown.

The soft glow of the lamp cast its gentle illumination over them. Shadows and golden highlights flitted capriciously over their bodies as they merged together.

Tony smiled as he buried his hand in the luxuriant silkiness of her hair. "I must be the luckiest man alive," he said softly. "I don't deserve your love after the things I've done, the things I've said."

"That's right, you don't," Lisa said promptly. A teasing smile tugged at the corners of her mouth. "You're altogether a first-rate stinker and I'm much too good for you." Her fingers began a provocative journey over his chest.

An answering grin broke over Tony's face like a light suddenly flashing. There was genuine happiness in his eyes, a confidence and satisfaction that Lisa had not seen before which thrilled and gratified her. His arms tightened around her, drawing her closer.

"But you love me in spite of it," he said forcefully.

Lisa nodded and her fingers went up to stroke his chin. "Yes, heaven help me."

"Why?"

Delicately, she shrugged her bare shoulders. "Beats me," she said with a laugh. A twinkle glittered in her eyes, turning them into sparkling emeralds. "Maybe I just have a penchant for men who rescue mermaids and despise journalists. Or maybe . . ." Her fingers stole up to trace the outline of his sensual lips.

"Maybe?" His mouth moved against her finger and he nibbled at it.

"Maybe I'm just a pushover for deep-brown eyes and kisses that send tingles shooting through me."

"Tingles?"

"Right down to my toes."

Tony's lips twitched. "Is that good?"

"It depends."

"On what?"

"On what happens after that," she replied, keeping a straight face. "If the tingles turn into electricity, that's good, but if they just fizzle away, that's bad."

"Hmmm. And what do I have to do to generate that flow of electricity?" he murmured. "This?" He bent his head to kiss her breast. "Or this?" A hand slid down her hip and around to stroke her sensitive inner thigh.

"Definitely," Lisa whispered as a shudder ran through her. Her eyelashes fluttered down while her hands slid up to cling to the hard strength of his shoulders.

Tony pressed her against the pillows and rained a torrent of kisses over her face. The tip of his tongue wreaked havoc over her as it explored the interior of her mouth with eager hunger, tracked the outline of her lips and teased her ear. Then his mouth returned once more to plunder hers.

His kisses had a drugging effect on Lisa, so that he became the opiate, she its hapless victim. Her mind floated, high and free, while her body's reflexes responded with a will of their own that was entirely independent of ordinary thought processes.

Slowly and with calculated deliberation, Tony aroused

her with his expert touch. His hands gently cupped her breasts before moving on to explore the undulating curve of her hips and thighs. Sparks of fire fanned through her until a delicious warmth radiated into every vein, every nerve, every cell. When his lips followed the trail of his fingers, the tension within Lisa built rapidly to an intolerable level.

"Oh, Tony," she murmured brokenly.

He lifted his head and his eyes, soft with desire, teased her. "Tingles?" he asked.

She shook her head. "Electricity," she gasped. "No question about it." Suddenly her eyes smoldered with sizzling heat, and in a flash she writhed out of his grasp and pushed him downward. "My turn," she stated with firm resolution.

A tiny smile parted Tony's lips as he lay quiescent, allowing her to have her way. Lisa bent over him and the tips of her breasts brushed tantalizingly across his chest.

"Close your eyes," she ordered softly.

He did so and Lisa bent lower still, kissing his eyelids, his forehead, his jaw and chin, before going on to tease his lips. There she lingered, catching his lower lip with her teeth, then using her tongue to probe the moist recesses beyond. She did all this without touching him with her hands, caressing the rugged planes of his face with only her lips and that as lightly, as fleetingly, as the quick strokes of a watercolor artist's brush strokes on rice parchment.

She felt him tremble as she inched downward to his throat and chest, still with the same feather-soft kisses as before. When her lips found the place just above his heart, she could feel its vibrant pounding, strong and fast. An exhilarating sense of power swelled within Lisa as she became aware of his heightened stimulation at each new move she made. She enjoyed the taste of him as her lips continued their erotic exploration of his hard, muscular chest.

Abruptly, Tony uttered a moan, lifted his arms and wrapped them around her. He pulled her down on top of him, holding her with the fierce strength of ardor. "You're trying to send me over the brink of sanity," he accused roughly. "But if I'm going to go out of my mind, you're going with me!"

To prove he meant it, he flipped her over onto her back and began a devastating assault on her senses. Lisa's blood raced furiously as he aroused her breasts with his mouth while his hands brought a pulsating, white-hot aching to her thighs.

A fierce, wild streak sprang alive within Lisa. Her hands went around his waist and her fingernails raked across his back, as a craving, sharp and raw, sliced through all layers of her consciousness, laying waste to acquired civility while resurrecting a deeply entrenched primitive passion. A powerful urgency shook her and she arched her body toward him, her proud feminity insisting that its needs be met.

Her uninhibited aggressiveness was like a torch to dry wood. Tony renewed his pillaging attack on her emotions, refusing, even yet, to give in to her demands. He was setting the pace and insatiably he plied her with kisses while his hands came to know her with ravaging thoroughness.

The pain of her privation was excruciating. Lisa made a small whimpering sound, knowing she could not hold on much longer, yet knowing, too, that she was completely susceptible to Tony's mood and could only wait for him to end the intimate torture.

Then he came down over her. His hands slid beneath her hips, fitting her to him. Eagerly, Lisa accepted him, anxious for a release from the fever that gripped her.

They moved together, slowly at first, but with a gradual increase in tempo as they began the exciting climb toward the summit of their passion. They clung to each other so tightly that even their hearts seemed fused, united with a single beat.

The release, when it finally came, was violent, sweeping over them like a gigantic tidal wave, transporting them to another dimension where only ecstasy reigned.

Tony lifted Lisa to him, with his hands at her back. His breathing was hard and his chest rose and fell against her breasts. Then they both sank weakly to the pillows, their bodies moist as they still held each other while they slowly descended from the blissful heights.

Moving to lay beside her, Tony inhaled deeply, gradually regaining control over his breathing. Then he turned on his side to face her and reached out to lift her hand. The tenderest expression Lisa had ever seen came into his eyes and softened his lips.

"I love you with all my heart," he said huskily. "Lisa, darling . . . will you marry me?"

After what had just happened between them, so perfect, so beautiful, Lisa hadn't imagined that she had the capacity for still more happiness. Yet now she found that she did. It spread over her like a warm, cozy blanket.

A smile quivered on her lips as she lifted a hand and caressed his jaw.

"Tony, darling . . . when?"

He caught her to him and his breath was soft and warm on her face. "As soon as we can arrange it," he said. "Next week?"

Lisa gave a tiny laugh. "Don't you think that's rushing it a little? There's no time to plan and my parents will never forgive me if I don't let them give me a proper wedding, no matter how simple."

Tony kissed the delicately shaped fingers he held and then grinned. "It's just that I'm so anxious for you to really be mine. But I guess that wouldn't be fair to your family and I don't want to get on their bad side even before they meet me," he added with an even broader grin. "A month, then? I don't think I could wait much more than that."

"It's a date!" Lisa smiled. "Mom will fuss, but she can manage in that amount of time." She leaned forward to kiss him lightly, but then she became serious. "Tony, are you sure you really want this? We haven't known each other very long. There's still so much we don't even know about each other yet and I don't want you to have any regrets or—"

"Hush!" he said in a gruff voice. "I won't even listen to such heresy. I know the most important fact about you, that you're a warm and wonderful person and that I desperately need you in my life. But what about you? Do you still have doubts?''

"Hush!" she ordered, just as he had done to her. "I've never been more certain about anything than I am about my feelings for you. The only thing that could possibly make me happier than I am this minute would be to become your wife.''

"Wouldn't you," he asked in an oddly wistful voice, ''be happy about becoming a mother one day, too? I want children, Lisa. I want to have a real family and give my children all the love I didn't have when I was young.''

"Of course I want children," she told him with a soft smile. "Your children," she added a little dreamily. Then she laughed gently. "But I have a sneaky suspicion that I'll have my hands full trying to keep you from spoiling them.''

Tony chuckled. "You may be right. I'll want to give them everything because they'll be a part of you." His eyes glowed as he gazed at her adoringly and he was no longer laughing as he promised, "I'll be a good father to them, and a good husband to you. When I say my vows to you, Lisa, I'll mean every word . . . for all time." He gave her a long kiss that while devoid of the passion that had ruled them earlier, was instead a sweet pledge for the rest of their lives.

The sun was already high in the sky and its light streamed in through the bedroom window when Lisa awoke the next morning. The space beside her was empty, but the indented pillow and thrown-back covers testified that another had shared the bed during the night.

She stretched and yawned and had just settled back against the pillows, dwelling on the momentous events of the night before, when the bedroom door opened.

Tony entered, looking outrageously appealing in snug denim jeans and a blue chambray shirt, opened at the neck with sleeves rolled up to the elbows. His thick dark hair was neatly combed and his face bore no hint of an overnight growth of beard. The fresh look of him combined with the vitality that was evident in his step made Lisa aware that she'd not only slept indecently late, but that she was also sleepy-faced with mussed hair. She was also acutely conscious that beneath the bedcovers she still wore not a single stitch.

"Good morning," Tony said heartily as he approached the bed. He carried a thick mug. "I brought you some coffee."

"Thanks." Holding the covers above her breasts with one hand, Lisa turned and propped up the pillows behind her head. "What time is it?" she asked as she settled back and accepted the cup.

"A little past nine." The mattress sagged as Tony sat down on the edge of the bed. He grinned wickedly. "Being an engaged woman seems to have made you a sleepyhead. Or was it the strenuous activity last night that made you so tired?"

To Lisa's horror, she felt herself actually blushing and quickly lowered her gaze to her coffee.

Tony noticed at once, of course, and laughed at her.

"Hey, you're not going to turn shy on me now, are you, tiger lady?"

"Stop it!" Lisa ordered, sounding irritable. "It's too early in the morning to be teased."

Tony tucked a finger beneath her chin and lifted her face, forcing her to look at him. His eyes twinkled as he asked softly, "Is it too early in the morning for a man to kiss his fiancée? Or to tell her how much he loves her?" Without waiting for a reply, he leaned forward to kiss her.

It was such a thoroughly satisfactory kiss that Lisa forgot her awkwardness. Though she still balanced the coffee in one hand, she lifted the other and threaded it through his hair while her soft lips parted beneath the sweet gentle pressure of his. When Tony drew back to smile at her, she was smiling, too.

His hand traced the edge of the blanket just above the swell of her breasts. "That was some kiss," he said a little unsteadily. "I'd better get out of here right now or I'll forget everything else except the fact that you're not wearing anything under those covers and how much I want to make love to you."

His light touch on her skin was already doing delightful things to her. Lisa closed her eyes, feeling warm and languorous and not at all ready to see him leave. "Then why don't you just forget everything else?" she murmured suggestively.

"Hmmm, maybe I will at that," he whispered in a thick voice. "Who cares if it makes Maggie mad when the breakfast gets cold?"

Lisa's eyes flew open, her mood instantly changed. "Maggie! I'd forgotten about her! Tony, I can't go out there and face her, knowing she knows—'' She broke off, frozen with embarrassment and dread.

''That we slept together last night?'' Tony asked. When Lisa nodded, he squeezed her hand. ''She's a big girl and she's not shocked or judgmental. Besides, I told her we're getting married. She approves,'' he added with a smile, ''and even told me she thinks I exhibited good sense in winning you. Now come on, darling. Get dressed and come eat. After that we've got to call your parents. We'll fly out to visit them next weekend so they can look me over. I only hope they like me half as much as Maggie likes you.''

''Don't be silly,'' Lisa chided. ''Of course they'll like you.''

Fifteen minutes later, Lisa left the shelter of the bedroom and went to the kitchen. In spite of Tony's assurances, she felt nervous about seeing Maggie. But Maggie herself made the moment easy. When Lisa walked into the room, she came over and gave her a hug.

''Welcome to the family, my dear. I couldn't be happier for Tony.''

''Thanks, Maggie.''

''You know, I've worried about Tony for years. Bachelor status may seem glamorous and carefree, but I've always known he was lonely and I kept hoping he would find the right girl.'' Maggie's eyes were serious. ''I think you are that girl and I'm very glad he found you.''

''I'm glad I found her, too,'' Tony said, sliding his arm possessively around Lisa's waist. He gazed down at her and asked half-seriously, ''Do we really have to wait a whole month for the wedding?''

"Of course you do!" Maggie said firmly. "How do you expect us to get everything done in less time? There are invitations to be printed, Lisa's dress, photographs for the paper, the cake, the church, the organist, the—"

Tony threw up his hands in defeat and grinned sheepishly. "Okay, okay. A month." He grinned at Lisa. "Unless you want to elope?"

"It sure would be a lot less trouble," she agreed, laughing. "I have to admit I hadn't thought of all those things."

"The bride and groom never do," Maggie said, shaking her head. "They always have their heads up in the clouds. That's what God invented mothers for . . . to attend to all the details. Now sit down and eat your breakfast, both of you, and when you call your parents, Lisa, don't hang up before I have a chance to speak with your mother. If both of us get organized and split the work load down the middle, maybe we'll get everything done in time."

Tony and Lisa sat down and then they both burst out laughing at the way Maggie was taking charge. Already, their own wedding seemed to have been taken out of their hands.

By two o'clock that afternoon, a lot of decisions had been made. Lisa's parents, surprised and excited at the news, had a long conversation with Tony that seemed to sway them favorably to the fact that their only daughter was about to marry a man they'd never met. Lisa's mother and Maggie spent forty-five minutes discussing plans. A color scheme was chosen, both older women promised to go to work immediately on their guest lists and Maggie's son Bill was called and enlisted to be the best man. Lisa would, of course, ask Roni to be her maid of honor. Beyond that, she was left with little more to do than shop for her wedding gown while Tony planned the honeymoon.

It was almost four when Tony walked with Lisa to her car. She was going home now because in the morning she had an interview scheduled. Tony would stay another night at the ranch so he could visit with Maggie before she left for San Francisco the next day.

"I wish you could stay," he told Lisa as he stowed her overnight bag in the backseat of her car.

"I wish I could, too," she replied. "I have this awful feeling that when I leave, I'll find I've only been dreaming."

Tony's arms circled her waist. "It's real all right," he whispered huskily. "I'm never going to let you go." He sighed. "I'd rather be going back with you, darling, but I feel I owe it to Maggie to stay until she leaves."

"Of course you have to stay," Lisa told him quickly. "I understand that. I guess"—she gave a little shrug and smiled wistfully—"I'm just missing you already."

Tony smiled warmly. "Same here." He kissed her forehead. "Tomorrow afternoon you'd better be ready to go shopping for an engagement ring as soon as I arrive. I'll feel a lot more confident once my ring is on your finger."

They kissed and continued to embrace each other,

reluctant to part. But at last Lisa withdrew from his arms, got into the car and, while Tony watched, drove out of sight.

That evening Roni and Jack celebrated with Lisa by opening a bottle of champagne. Excited and genuinely happy for her, Roni seemed as bubbly as the champagne. "I can't believe it! You're actually going to be married before me!"

Lisa shook her head. "I'm not sure I believe it either."

"Hey," Jack scolded. "For a bride-to-be, you sure do look down in the dumps all of a sudden. What's the matter? Having second thoughts?"

"No, not that," Lisa said. "I guess everything's happening so fast, I'm still in a state of shock."

"I know what's the matter with her," Roni said shrewdly.

"What's that, love?" Jack asked.

"She's just depressed because Tony isn't here with her tonight."

At that moment the telephone rang and Roni sprang to her feet and went to answer it. A satisfied grin came to her face as she held out the phone to Lisa and said, "There's this man on the line who sounds lovesick and lonely and needs somebody to cheer him up."

"Tony?" Lisa hurried to the phone and when she heard his voice, the melancholy that had been slowly mounting ever since she had left the ranch that afternoon abruptly disappeared. A sparkle came to her eyes and a smile to her lips.

Roni turned to Jack and laughed. "I told you I knew

what was wrong with her. Do you get the feeling that our company isn't stimulating enough for her?"

"Positively," Jack replied. He got swiftly to his feet. "Come on, honey, let's go out to the kitchen and give her a little privacy."

Lisa was grateful for their consideration as she sank into the easy chair next to the phone.

"I'm missing you dreadfully," Tony said in a deep voice.

"I miss you, too." Lisa's throat ached. "More than I can possibly say."

Tony chuckled. "Since you left, the hours have dragged by and I've behaved so badly that Maggie has threatened to disown me if I don't start showing a little more enthusiasm for her company."

Lisa laughed huskily. "I'm the same way. Jack and Roni have been trying to help me celebrate, but I've been moping so much I think Jack's decided he wasted his money on the champagne. I wish," she ended softly, "that you were here with us."

"I don't," Tony said, surprising her before he continued. "I wish I had you all alone to myself so that I could hold you and kiss you and make love to you."

"Oh, Tony," she said shakily, "I'm beginning to think you were right about getting married next week. A whole month seems like a lifetime away."

"*Tomorrow* is a lifetime away," he corrected. He laughed suddenly. "You know, I'm amazed at my own impatience. I never felt this way before . . . that all of life has come to a standstill until I can be with one strawberry-blond mermaid again."

Lisa laughed, too. "Whoever said 'Love is hell' was right. It's sheer torture."

"It sure is. Except for a few shining moments, I've been utterly miserable ever since I met you," Tony complained.

"It's no more than you deserve," she teased, "for making me miserable, too."

The tone of his voice altered, becoming soft and intimate. "Dream about me tonight?"

"I promise," Lisa said, "if you'll do the same."

Tony chuckled again. "I probably won't get any sleep at all because I'll be too busy thinking about you and about how lonely the bed is without you in it. I'll let you go for now, darling. Remember that I love you and I'll see you tomorrow just as soon as I can get there."

"I'll be waiting. Good night, Tony."

The next morning Lisa awoke with joy in her heart. The long night was over and now only hours remained until she would be reunited with Tony. It was amazing how he now completely dominated every aspect of her life. Thoughts of him colored everything. In short, her world revolved around him. Nothing else mattered.

When she flipped over to glance at her bedside clock, she decided something else had better matter. It was seven-thirty, she had overslept and if she didn't get a move on, she would be late for her interview. She had lined up an appointment with a young TV actor whose hobby was sky-diving, which was to be the subject of her article, and their meeting was scheduled for nine o'clock on the set at the film studio. Lisa bounded out of bed and dashed for the bathroom.

Roni had overslept also and Lisa had to wake her. Then both girls rushed madly to get dressed and out of the apartment. There was no time for the normal morning routine of coffee and breakfast.

Lisa was ready to leave first. On her way out, she found the morning newspaper at the door, and hastily picked it up and tossed it on the sofa. Then she dashed down the stairs and out to her car to begin the drive to Burbank.

She was fifteen minutes late for her meeting, but fortunately it didn't cause any problems. There seemed to be some trouble with the electrical wiring on the set, and while repairmen worked on it the actors and production crew of the series were taking a break. Lisa and the actor she was interviewing sat in an out-of-the-way corner of the studio where they were able to talk without interruption.

It went well and by the time Lisa left, she felt pleased and optimistic that she would have an interesting story. The actor himself had been likable, friendly and enthusiastic about his subject. Before they parted, Lisa arranged for him to meet on the following Saturday with a freelance photographer she often used for a photo session.

It was almost noon when she got home and Lisa was both tired and hungry. She made herself a sandwich, poured a glass of milk and sat down at the kitchen table to eat while she went through the mail and belatedly read the morning paper.

She was pleased to find a check from a business journal

for an article she'd done about a woman realtor's success, another from a nature magazine for a piece about the redwoods and a letter from the editor of another magazine approving a query idea she'd sent and suggesting yet another. Lisa chuckled to herself as she tucked the letter back into the envelope. It seemed as though, suddenly, when love went right so did everything else. At the moment her career and financial situation were in better shape than they had been in some time, even without the job at *Today's Journal* she'd wanted so badly.

Lisa ate slowly as she picked up the newspaper and looked at the front page. It was filled with the usual: the federal deficit, more worries about rising interest rates, violence in the Middle East, a drug smuggler arrested.

She flipped the page, her eyes scanning the headlines, and then her heart literally stopped. There, on page two, above the wire service story, were the words "Ex-Football Pro Donates Million to Needy Kids."

She read the article hastily. It had all the essential facts concerning Tony's donation all right, complete with the additional information that he'd wanted it to remain a secret. Then had come a brief but hard-hitting description of his past fame as a ballplayer, his aversion to the press and, of course, a mention of the court case involving Carmen Woods.

When she folded the paper and shoved it away, Lisa had a sick feeling in the pit of her stomach and a chill of foreboding snaked its way up her back.

Chapter Eleven

*W*hen Tony had neither arrived nor telephoned by three o'clock that afternoon, Lisa knew he had seen the newspaper article. She knew, too, that he must think she had given out the information to the wire service. A sense of dread spread through her and ice water now flowed in her veins, frigid and numbing. She couldn't move, couldn't think what to do, was only scarcely breathing. Was it, then, to end this way . . . with this awful wall of silence?

But suddenly her blood flowed hot again. She wouldn't let it happen. Their love . . . their future was at stake and she could not sit by passively and do nothing to save it.

Trembling but determined, Lisa went into the bedroom to comb her hair and apply a fresh coat of lipstick. She noted automatically that she looked neat enough in her cream-colored skirt and blue silk blouse, but when her gaze lifted to her face, she got a jolt. It was colorless and there was a dark, haunted look about her eyes. She steadied herself as best she could, dabbed a heavier-than-usual coat of blusher to her cheeks and finally, with a feeling of doom that she couldn't shake, picked up her purse and let herself out of the apartment.

Once she reached the office building, for a moment Lisa's nerve failed her. But the knowledge that she had done nothing wrong braced her, renewed her courage, and she went inside and stepped into the elevator.

In the suite of offices that Tony occupied, Lisa went without any hesitation to his secretary's desk. As soon as she announced her name, a strange expression came over the other girl's face.

"I'm sorry, Miss Knight," she said quickly, "but Mr. Neugent is in conference and can't be disturbed. If you'd care to leave a message, I'll be sure and—"

"He gave you orders not to put through any calls I might make or let me in to see him, didn't he?" Lisa interrupted bluntly.

The other girl looked taken aback and stuttered, "I—I really can't . . . ."

Lisa took pity on her. "It's not your fault," she said kindly. "You were only doing your duty. Nevertheless, I *am* going to see him." With deliberate steps, she went past the desk to the door beyond.

"Wait a minute!" the secretary exclaimed, rising from her chair. "You can't go in there!"

Lisa gave her a brittle smile and firmly twisted the doorknob. "Watch me," she said softly.

When she opened the door, she saw Tony at once,

seated at his desk, head bent as he studied some graphs. The sound of the door made him glance up and when he saw her standing there, a look of blank astonishment crossed his face.

From behind Lisa, she heard the secretary's anxious voice. "I'm terribly sorry, Mr. Neugent, but she just took it upon herself to come in and—"

Tony had risen from behind the desk and the expression of surprise had already given way to one of swift, dark anger. He nodded curtly and said in a voice of steel, "It's all right, Julie. I understand." He gave Lisa a cold look and said, "Now that you're in, you may as well sit down." He glanced back at his secretary, adding, "Close the door, will you? And don't interrupt me with any calls."

Lisa stepped into the room, only dimly aware of the door closing behind her. Her nerves tensed while her eyes never left Tony's face. It was grim and his jaw was hard, like marble. His eyes glinted, two black stones, and his mouth was a well-defined slash of resentment and fury. His entire body was taut, like a soldier about to march into battle. His stance was hostile and intimidating, and even before she voiced a single word, Lisa felt utter hopelessness sweep over her. It was abundantly clear that he didn't want to hear anything she had to say, and with a sinking sensation, she wondered if it was any use even to try.

But of course she had to try. It was why she had come, to convince him of her innocence. And he *had* to believe her! The alternative was unthinkable. She swallowed with difficulty and her voice, when it came, was scarcely above a whisper. "Tony, I came to—"

"Rub it in?" he interrupted savagely.

"No!" she cried out. She held out a trembling hand toward him, unconsciously pleading.

"No?" He ignored her hand as well as the pain in her voice. "I can't imagine what other reason brought you here. Surely," he added with contempt, "you can't expect me to still have any desire to marry you?"

"Tony, I love you!"

His mouth twisted into a bitter grin. "You have the oddest way of showing it," he said sarcastically. "I hope that you were well paid for your treachery."

Lisa sucked in a ragged breath. "I'm trying to tell you, I didn't give out that information to the press. I would never go behind your back and betray you like that!" Her voice broke over the words.

Tony muttered a curse and without warning covered the short distance between them. His hands shot out and gripped her shoulders roughly. His fingers dug into the tender flesh beneath her blouse.

"I can't believe your incredible nerve!" he exclaimed harshly. "It's there in black and white in half the newspapers in the country and you're trying to lie to me and say you didn't do it when you're the one who was so dead set on writing about me? Give me credit for a little sense! I've been gullible where you're concerned, but I'm not that stupid!"

Abruptly his hands fell away from her and when their gazes collided, Lisa was taken aback. Tony despised her and she was sickened by the revulsion that was so transparent in his eyes.

As though he were suddenly weary of the whole

situation, Tony turned his back to her and leaned forward as he braced his hands on the edge of his desk. His head was bent and his voice dull and lacking any inflection at all as he said, ''Just . . . please go, Lisa.''

Lisa's heart ached as she looked at his rigid back and hot tears burned her eyes. Slowly, she moved to stand directly behind him.

''Why won't you believe me?'' she whispered. ''Tony, if you love me, then you have to trust me!''

He whirled around to glare at her. ''Love?'' He spit out the word as though it were something dirty. ''There's no such thing! I should have realized that long ago, but like an idiot, I kept hoping and you fooled me enough that for a while I really believed in it. But I'm no longer a fool. My trust in you was misplaced and I'm not likely to ever make that kind of mistake again!''

Lisa straightened her shoulders and though she was half blinded by the tears that filled her eyes, she gathered her dignity about her. ''I see,'' she said quietly. ''Then there's nothing more to be said.''

For a strange, timeless moment, they gazed at one another. Through the rainbow mist of tears that she tried hard to blink away, Lisa allowed herself the indulgence of looking at him for the last time. Pride forbade her from begging him to believe her, that and the knowledge that without trust, they had, in truth, never had anything at all. Even so, she stood motionless for one instant longer so that her eyes could memorize his face.

Oddly, as she looked at him, mentally storing away all the little details about him—the exact angle that his dark hair fell across the right side of his forehead, the way the laugh lines etched delicate, upward-sweeping grooves from the edges of his eyes or the square cut of his strong jaw—Tony seemed to be studying her in the same manner. For this brief span of time while they looked at each other, the anger faded and only regret, on both their parts, was apparent.

Then Lisa broke the spell. "Good-bye, Tony," she said in as level a voice as she could manage.

He nodded briefly. "Good-bye, Lisa."

Before she broke down entirely, Lisa turned and hurried from the room. When she was within the frame of the doorway, she thought she heard him call her name, but the sound was so faint she could not be sure and she didn't dare stop to find out. Her throat was choked with unshed tears that stung her eyes. She had to get away completely . . . and fast.

Why had he tried to call her back like that? Tony wondered, angry at himself. Just because she'd looked forlorn and desolate for a moment, as though she really did love him, he had weakened. But once the door was closed, shutting her out of view, he'd been glad she hadn't responded. As Lisa herself had pointed out, there was nothing else to be said.

But that didn't eliminate the pain that seared through his chest like a branding iron. He loved her so much it was almost like a sickness with him. When he'd seen that write-up in the paper when he'd stopped for breakfast at a small cafe on his way back from the ranch this morning, he had felt as though the very ground had caved in beneath his feet. He wasn't sure he would ever get over the fact that money had meant more to her than he had. She'd lied to him about loving him and she'd lied when she'd said she wouldn't write about him. True, this hadn't been a magazine article, as she'd originally intended, but he supposed she must have been well paid for the information she'd supplied the news service. The selfishness and deceit of women continued to astonish him, and with self-contempt, he wondered if he would ever learn they couldn't be trusted. First there'd been his mother, then Carmen, and now, in a way that was worse even than the abandonment of his mother, there was Lisa.

A soft knock sounded at the door. Tony's heart stopped. Had she come back after all?

"Come in," he barked.

The door opened and instead of the face he had been half hoping, half afraid he would see, it was that of his secretary. She approached him warily, as though he were a bomb about to detonate.

"I really am sorry about letting Miss Knight in," Julie apologized again. "But she went right past me and there was nothing I could do to stop her."

"I know. I told you it was all right. What's that?" He nodded, indicating the papers in her hand.

"Phone messages that came while you were, ah, occupied with Miss Knight. Mr. Gillis of the Cameron Children's Foundation called again to apologize once more about the news leak and to say he's working on finding out who did it. He says when he does, the individual responsible will be fired."

Thinking it would be Roni who had told Lisa in the first place, Tony groaned. The damage had already been done and in his opinion no good would come of sacking anyone. "I'll call him back immediately," he said. "A reprimand is certainly in order, but I don't want to cost anyone their job."

Julie nodded. "It'll have to wait until morning, though. He won't be in his office the rest of the day."

"All right. Remind me tomorrow," Tony said briskly. "Any other calls?"

"Yes. Mrs. Borden called from San Francisco and she wants you to call her back. You can reach her at this number."

"Fine." Tony glanced at his watch and then dismissed her. "It's almost five. You may as well close up shop now, Julie. I'll see you in the morning."

Julie nodded. "Good night, sir." She handed him the paper with Maggie's telephone number and then quietly left the room.

Tony dialed the number at once and as soon as Maggie came on the line asked anxiously, "What's the matter? Did you have car trouble on the trip?"

"No, no, I made it just fine and Amy and I are making plans to go out for dinner this evening. I called," she went on, coming straight to the point, "because I saw the news item about you in the paper. You don't think it was Lisa, do you?"

"Of course it was Lisa," he grated harshly. "Who else would have done it?"

"Anyone who works at the foundation could have done it," Maggie said reasonably. "What does Lisa say?"

"She said she didn't do it," Tony said shortly, "but I don't believe her."

"Why not? The girl is crazy about you, Tony. She wouldn't do anything to hurt you."

"She already did," he snapped.

Maggie sighed. "Did you break off with her?"

"Naturally. I don't intend to marry a woman who tells me she loves me one minute and then stabs me in the back the next."

"You love her, don't you?"

"What's that got to do with anything?" Tony growled. "She's a liar! She can't be trusted!"

"Are you so sure about that?"

"Of course I'm sure!" Tony shouted. "Hell, can't you see that it just wouldn't matter that much if it were anybody else? True, I like my privacy and I don't like ancient sore points being dredged up in the press, but it's not as though I'm a criminal or have anything to hide. I can take the heat of publicity when I have to. What I can't take is Lisa's deceit. I can't forgive that, Maggie. Not ever."

"If she really did it, of course you can't, but I'm not convinced she did, Tony. One woman can usually spot the truth about another. And all I saw was how much Lisa loves you."

"You liked her," Tony pointed out sadly. "You saw what you wanted to see, the same as I did. But we were both mistaken."

When Lisa got home, Roni was just emerging from her bedroom where she'd changed out of her working clothes into a pair of shorts and a shirt. She took one penetrating look at Lisa's white face and said, without any need to have it confirmed, "Tony thinks you gave that story to the wire service."

Lisa nodded. "He wouldn't even listen to me, much less believe me when I said I didn't."

"The office was in an uproar about the leak," Roni told her, "and Mr. Gillis is determined to get to the bottom of it. He'll find out, Lisa, and when he does, he'll tell Tony the truth."

"It doesn't matter," Lisa said dully. "Tony and I are through. He hates me."

"But when he knows the truth . . ." Roni said urgently.

Lisa shook her head. "It won't change anything between us. I thought he loved me, Roni, but when you love someone, you have to trust them, believe in them, give them the benefit of the doubt. Tony has always assumed the worst about me first and asked questions later. What kind of relationship could we possibly have based on a complete lack of faith on his part? It would never work and I realized that this afternoon when he refused to accept my word."

"I'm sorry," Roni said softly. "I'm really sorry, Lisa."

Lisa managed a wry smile. "So am I." In a different tone, she said, "Roni, I have to get away for a while and sort things out."

"Get away? Where?"

Lisa shrugged with indifference. "Wherever the mood strikes me."

"How long will you be gone?" Roni persisted, looking suddenly anxious.

"I don't know that, either," Lisa said in a lifeless voice. "A few days, a few weeks, however long it takes to figure out what I'm going to do with myself from this point on. All I know right now is that I need a change, a real change."

"When will you go?"

"In the morning. I got a couple of checks in the mail today and I'll need to stop by the bank before I leave." She sighed heavily. "I guess I'd better call my parents now and tell them to forget the wedding plans." She laughed bitterly. "Do you suppose I could win the prize for having the shortest engagement on record?"

Roni ignored the sarcasm. "I wish I could talk you out of this trip," she said. "I don't like the idea of you just heading off someplace without anybody knowing where you are or when you're coming back. Your parents wouldn't like it any better than I do," she added pointedly.

"I don't suppose they would," Lisa agreed, "but I'm a big girl and I can take care of myself. Don't worry about me. I'll be fine."

"Sez you," Roni retorted. As Lisa reached for the telephone, she went toward the kitchen to start their supper.

The following morning the two girls hugged each other and said a tearful good-bye before Roni left for her job.

"Call me when you get where you're going," Roni insisted. "At least let me know where you are."

Lisa grimaced. "I'll call to let you know I'm all right, but I won't tell you where I am."

Roni's eyes widened. "Why not?"

"Because if Tony wants to contact me after he learns the truth, I don't want you to be able to tell him where I am."

"I wouldn't tell," Roni said indignantly. "I know how to keep a secret."

"Yes," Lisa answered, "but it's better this way. Tony can be very persuasive when he wants to be. Besides, if you really don't know, then you won't have to lie about anything."

After Roni left, Lisa packed the remaining last-minute items she needed and by nine o'clock her bag and her portable typewriter were stowed away in her car. After a quick trip to the bank, she was on her way.

The smog was heavy, spreading its suffocating blanket over the city. To Lisa it was fitting, for it matched the oppressive, heavy unhappiness that lay over her heart. Someday, perhaps, the wound would heal and she might be able to love again, but she didn't really believe that. The hurt went far too deep. Her very soul would always bear the scar.

Tony, too, had been hurt by this, but the difference between them was that he had brought the pain on himself as well as on her because he simply couldn't find it in him to trust anyone. Or at least not her, Lisa amended to herself. He trusted Maggie in the sense that she trusted her own parents, but that was hardly the same. Tony trusted no one else and Lisa sorrowfully acknowledged that it was unlikely he ever would. It had been bred into him from an early age that he could believe in the security of no one except himself, that the people he loved always betrayed him. There was no way she could fight his past and win. The shadow of it would always be there, erecting a wall of suspicion between them and no matter how much she loved him, Lisa knew with certainty that she could never endure a lifetime of fighting doubts and mistrust. It went against the very nature of her being.

It was after ten A.M. when Tony arrived at his office. He was haggard from lack of sleep and he knew he looked as awful as he felt. At first light this morning he'd been out walking the beach, fighting the devil in himself that tortured him unmercifully. In spite of what she had done, in spite of the proof of her duplicity, he could not shake off the strange hurt that had been in Lisa's eyes yesterday just before she left him. The expression in them haunted him.

Julie was not at her desk when he passed it to reach his own office, but when he sat down at his desk he saw that she'd placed a small stack of phone messages on it. Tony quickly shuffled through them and decided to return Gillis's call from the Cameron Children's Foundation first.

He reached the man immediately and Bob Gillis, sounding abject, said, "I'm sorry I couldn't get hold of you yesterday, Tony. I can't apologize enough for the news leak about your donation. But this morning I learned who was responsible and I've given the young man two weeks' notice."

"That's all right. I wanted to let you know that I—"

Tony stopped abruptly as the other man's words penetrated. "Did you say 'young man'?"

"Yes. What happened is that he had a few drinks at a party one night. Unfortunately, while his tongue was loose, he happened to be talking to someone who works for the wire service. He's really sorry about the whole thing, but that's beside the point, of course."

Tony felt as though a heavy-set, rock-hard tackle had just knocked him off his feet on a football field. His head reeled and he couldn't seem to breathe. What had he done? he thought frantically. *What in God's name had he done?* Lisa had been telling him the truth!

"Tony, are you still there?"

Tony gathered his chaotic thoughts and hoped he sounded normal. "Yes, I'm still here. Thanks for telling me. And by the way, give the fellow back his job."

"You don't want me to fire him?" Gillis asked, sounding amazed.

Tony felt suddenly magnanimous now that he knew Lisa had not been dishonest. He laughed shortly and said, "Give him a raise for all I care. Just don't trust him with any more secrets."

As soon as they rang off, Tony sprang from his seat, grabbed the suit jacket he'd just hung on the coatrack and strode out of the office. Julie was just entering hers, carrying two mugs of coffee, one for him, one for herself.

"Good morning," she said.

"Good-bye," Tony said as he shrugged into his jacket. "I'm going out and I'm not sure when I'll be back. Break any appointments I had for the day, okay?"

Julie stared at him in confusion. Then she merely nodded and said calmly, "Whatever you say."

Tony drove straight to Lisa's apartment and felt a surge of wild frustration when she didn't answer the door. He raced down the stairs and searched in the parking area for her car. He didn't find it and when he returned to his own car he hit the hood with his fist.

Five minutes later he stopped at the first service station he came to and, using the public telephone, called the Cameron Children's Foundation for the second time that morning. This time he asked for Roni and when she came on the line, he didn't waste any time with pleasantries.

"This is Tony Neugent," he told her. "I need to find Lisa and she's not at home. Do you know where she is?"

"No, I don't. She went away."

"Away?" Shock waves rippled through Tony. "What do you mean? Where did she go?"

"You've spoken with Mr. Gillis this morning, haven't you?" Roni said shrewdly. "And now you know who leaked the story to the press about your donation."

"Yes, yes," Tony said impatiently. "Tell me where Lisa went so I can find her."

"I told you, I honestly don't know. She knew you'd find out the truth and she didn't want you to be able to reach her when you did," Roni said bluntly, "so she wouldn't even tell me where she was going or when she was coming back. I'm really sorry, Tony, but I don't think she wants anything more to do with you . . . ever."

A chill of defeat crept up Tony's spine. He knew Roni spoke nothing less than the truth. "I . . . see," he said huskily. "I can't blame her. But no matter how she feels about me now, I have to apologize to her even if she won't have me back. When you talk to her, tell her, tell her—" He broke off, unable to go on.

"I will," Roni said softly. "For what it's worth, if you want my opinion, I don't believe you should give up without a fight. If you care enough to try, that is."

"I care," Tony assured her. He cleared his throat. "But after this, I'm not sure she ever will again."

Chapter Twelve

$\mathcal{L}$ isa stood on the redwood deck of her uncle's vacation home overlooking beautiful Lake Tahoe. The oval-shaped glacier-formed lake, nestled in a valley between the ragged mountain peaks of the Sierra Nevada range and lush green pine forests, was a spectacular sight. As dusk began to fall, the mountains and trees cast their dark shadows across the deepening blue of the water. In spite of her unhappiness, Lisa was moved by the lovely grandeur. Her throat squeezed tight and tears burned her eyes. Overwhelming beauty always made her emotional.

The air was chilled as night came swiftly and Lisa hugged her arms about her. Soon the growing cold would drive her inside. She inhaled the sharp, fresh air and postponed as long as possible the moment when she would have to go indoors and be alone with herself and with her thoughts.

Yesterday, when she had not known where to turn, she had suddenly thought of her uncle's place here in the mountains. He was a widower who lived in Maryland and came to occupy it several times a year. The rest of the time it remained empty and when he had bought it four years ago, he had given Lisa a key of her own and issued her an open invitation to use it whenever she wished. A few times Lisa and Roni, along with other friends, had stayed there during the winter skiing season at Squaw Valley.

But this was far different from the other times she had come here. Then there had been warm companionship and the excitement of the ski slopes; now there was only herself, and as night closed in loneliness came with it. Until this moment she had escaped dealing with her thoughts or emotions by the simple expedient of being too numb and tired. Yesterday there had been the long drive up Interstate 5 and by the time she'd stopped at a motel in Sacramento to spend the night, she'd been trembling with fatigue and had fallen asleep without even bothering to go out for dinner. This morning she'd been up early for the remainder of the drive to the lake and after unloading her bags at her uncle's rustic vacation house, she had headed immediately for the water where she had walked along the shore for hours.

Although Tony had never been entirely out of her mind, there had been some sort of protective buffer shielding her from any direct confrontation, so that she saw him and what had happened through a diffused mental looking glass. Dispassionately, disassociated, a victim of shock, she had been able to accept the bare fact that their love was over. Her heart, though she didn't realize it yet, had not been able to believe it.

At last the cold and darkness drove Lisa indoors. She was exhausted from her long day of physical exertion, but it was her mental fatigue that was most debilitating. She suddenly realized she hadn't bothered to eat all day, so she made herself a salami and cheese sandwich. She had no appetite or ambition for something more palate-satisfying, and as it was she only nibbled at the sandwich.

The evening stretched out before her, bleak and empty. Lisa thought of driving over to Reno to spend the evening in one of the plush casinos there. She could try her luck at one of the gaming tables and perhaps take in a show. But almost as soon as she thought of it, she decided against it because it required too much effort. In the past such a diversion had been fun, but only because she had also had companionship. In her present mood, even if she were to win a huge jackpot it would fail to cheer her and she doubted the ability of even the most talented entertainer to please her tonight.

Restlessly, Lisa prowled the house, wishing she were back in Los Angeles, wishing she'd gone to visit her parents instead of coming here where the solitude she'd thought she wanted now closed in on her. Most of all she wished she could shake this strangely heavy, dull, zombielike state she was in.

Finally, she decided to take a shower and go to bed. Her limbs ached, her throat felt scratchy and dry and her eyes were moist and salty. She wondered if she was coming down with a virus. It seemed all she could do to step out of the shower, dry off and slip into her nightgown.

When she walked into the bedroom, the pain broke over her without warning, like the lashing rains of a violent Pacific storm. At last her heart admitted what it had been denying. Tony was lost to her for good, this was reality and somehow she had to get on with the business of living without him. Her love had not been enough for him and never could be. Suspicion and distrust had nothing to do with love, and while he had cared for her the feelings he'd had for her had not been genuine love. Perhaps he was incapable of it.

The storm took its toll and when it ended, weak and spent, Lisa fell asleep across the bed, too tired even to crawl between the covers.

She awoke very early on Wednesday morning. Though there was still a dull ache within her due to the emotional upheaval of the night before, she felt strangely calm and decisive. She needed a complete change, a cutting break with her past. There was nothing at all to keep her in Los Angeles. She had no permanent job to hold her back; besides, Roni would be married in just a few more months and then she would be alone anyway. Now was as good a time as any to make a new start someplace else.

Maybe Phoenix, she thought, giving it serious consideration. Her parents would be delighted to have her live nearby. She could find a job there to support herself and she could still continue her writing on a part-time basis, at night or on weekends. Lisa foresaw a lot of empty, lonely evenings ahead to fill.

She dressed and went into the kitchen to make coffee. While it was still early enough to catch Roni before she left for work, Lisa decided to call. "Hi, it's me," she said when Roni answered the phone.

"Are you all right?" Roni asked anxiously. "I thought you would have called before now."

"I meant to call you last night," Lisa said apologetically, "but I was tired and fell asleep early. And yes, I'm fine."

"Mr. Gillis found out who leaked the story," Roni said, going straight to the point. "It was one of the guys in the office. Rumor is Mr. Gillis fired him but Tony made him give him back his job."

"That's nice," Lisa said noncommittally.

"He called several times and came by last night and the night before," Roni offered. "He really looks horrible, Lisa, and he's desperate to talk to you. Why don't you call him and straighten this thing out?"

"Because there's nothing to straighten out."

"You're being too hard on him."

Lisa's mouth twisted wryly. "Whose side are you on?" she asked. "I know you mean well, but believe me, it's best to leave things the way they are."

"If you could see him, I think you'd change your mind," Roni said, "but it's your business. By the way, Maggie Borden has called twice. She wants you to call her back. I've got the number here someplace, or are you not talking to her, either?"

"There's no need for sarcasm," Lisa said. "Of course I'll call her back. What's the number?" She picked up a pencil.

Roni reeled it off and then, dropping the touchy subject of Tony altogether, they spoke of other things for a few minutes before ringing off.

Because she wasn't all that anxious to speak with Maggie, Lisa delayed the call until after she was fortified by two cups of coffee. She frowned at the piece of paper with the phone number, dreading to hear what she knew would be coming. Maggie, like Roni, would try to get her to call Tony, and because he was important to her, her arguments were bound to be more persuasive.

When she did call her, it was just as she had expected. Right away Maggie said, "Now tell me, dear, what is all this nonsense about you and Tony not getting married after all? If ever I met a couple who belong together, it's the two of you."

"Maggie, you should know that Tony is the one who broke things off."

"*Initially,* yes," Maggie conceded, but that was all she was allowing. "He was hurt and angry and he did it in the heat of the moment, but this running away of yours is just as bad. How can he possibly make amends when he can't even find you?"

Lisa sighed. "I can't see him. Don't you understand? If I do, I'll end up lowering my guard and will only be hurt again the next time around. It's happened before, so I know there'll be a next time and a next. I'm not strong enough to resist him and I must, for both our sakes. We're totally wrong for each other."

"If you love each other enough to work out your differences, how can it be wrong?"

"That's just it! There's no way of working out the

differences because Tony doesn't love me enough to trust me. Everything I seem to do or say is questionable and he always assumes the very worst. I can't face a future with a man who has absolutely no faith in me! Can you imagine what that would be like? Can you?'' She broke off, choking back tears.

There was a thoughtful silence before Maggie asked quietly, ''Do you love him enough to forgive him?''

''Forgive? It's not a question of forgiveness!'' Lisa cried. ''Of course I can forgive him. And I do love him, Maggie! You know that. But I can't endure his constant assumptions that I'm some sort of horrible monster out to stab him in the back!''

''I see. Perhaps you're not the right person for Tony after all,'' Maggie said. ''If you were, you'd be a little more tolerant and understanding of how difficult it is for him to trust anyone. And you'd be able to see just how far along the road to trust he's already come because of you.''

Lisa's fingers tightened around the receiver. ''What do you mean?''

''People have betrayed Tony all his life. First his father deserted him, then his mother. She even went so far as to make him lie and steal for her! Then one day when he was ten, she simply packed up and walked out while he was at school. Think how devastating that was to a little boy and how it might seriously impair his ability to trust in others! After that he was shuffled around like a piece of used furniture from foster home to foster home until one day Cal brought him home to me.''

''I know all that, Maggie,'' Lisa said softly. ''But he adores and trusts you.''

Maggie laughed, but it was a kindly sound. "You don't think such a rapport happened overnight, do you? In the beginning he was as suspicious of us as he was of anyone else. The only saving grace was that he liked football and he saw that Cal was a fair-minded coach with his team. I just sort of hung around the fringes and hoped one day he'd grow to tolerate me."

"How did you finally bring him around?" Lisa asked, genuinely curious.

"Oddly enough, it happened entirely by accident. The last few months of my pregnancy with Bill, Tony withdrew even more. I knew it was because he thought we wouldn't want him anymore once we had the baby, but he was so unapproachable I didn't quite know how to reassure him. But then the baby arrived a couple of weeks early while Cal was out of town visiting his mother, who was ill at the time. It was left up to Tony to get me to the hospital, call Cal and even handle all the hospital checking-in business while they rushed me up to the delivery room. There was no way Cal could get there before the baby was born and all my family lived too far away to come, of course, so Tony was the sole family representative in the waiting room the whole time. He was the first person who saw the baby after he was born, even before I did, and I think that did something to him, made him feel like Bill was part his in a way, that and the knowledge that he alone had been responsible for the baby's and my safety and that he'd handled the job just fine. That's a pretty heavy load for a sixteen-year-old boy, you know."

"Yes, I'd say it was." Lisa could visualize how anxious

he must have been to take care of Maggie properly; she could even imagine what thoughts must have gone through his head while he'd waited alone throughout the birth, feeling certain that the infant's arrival would rob him of the little security he had found in Maggie's and Cal's affections.

"The next day in my hospital room after Cal arrived," Maggie went on, "the three of us were discussing the excitement of it all and I happened to say I didn't know what I would have done without Tony. I remember Cal's exact words. He said, 'I hope we don't ever have to find out.' Then he told Tony, 'I depended on you to take care of your mother while I was gone, son, and you didn't let me down. I'm proud of you.' From that moment on, I think Tony felt he really did belong. That's when I really did become his mother and Cal his father, and instead of ever showing the least bit of jealousy over Bill's arrival, you'd have thought the baby was his own personal property, he was so proud of him. The two of them are very close to this day, despite the wide gap in their ages. What I'm trying to say, Lisa, is that in a strange sort of way, Tony had to first have faith in his own worth before he could quite trust in our love for him or in his for us."

"I understand what you're saying, Maggie, but this is a different situation altogether."

"Indeed it is, and more difficult, too, because while Tony learned to trust Cal and me, the unfortunate episode with Carmen later set him back all over again. She not only cheated on him while they were engaged, but then she had the nerve to take him to court and sue him to support a child that wasn't even his! Is it really any wonder that he has such a hard time believing in anyone? Especially a woman''—she chuckled—''and a woman journalist at that?''

"I . . . I suppose not," Lisa said slowly.

"Think over what I've said, dear," Maggie said gently. "Tony really does love you and need you. Very badly. I hope you won't let my boy down. That's happened to him enough already."

"Thanks, Maggie," Lisa said huskily. "Thanks a lot."

After they rang off, Lisa went outdoors to the deck. The morning sun was brilliant across the crystal lake. Mountain peaks were reflected on the still waters and the air was spicy with the scent of pine.

Lisa stood at the rail, gazing toward the glittering lake, but she scarcely saw it. She realized that Maggie had just handed her the key to understanding Tony in a way she never had before. She'd known his lack of trust stemmed from his childhood, but what she hadn't seen was the inferiority complex it had given him. In the eyes of the world, by its criteria, he was a smashing success. He'd been a famous, adored athlete and later on a prosperous, accomplished businessman. He seemed to have it all, a winner's streak of good fortune, the golden touch, everything such success can buy; but what no one had ever seen, including herself, was his well-concealed inability to believe himself deserving of the grandest prize of all . . . love. With Maggie and her family, he had found a measure of it at last, but in the normal next step of finding it with a woman, the treasure had eluded him, remaining buried beneath still more deceit and cruelty by the actress named Carmen.

It was little wonder, then, that Tony had been so quick to mistrust her and judge her so harshly. It wasn't because he didn't love her . . . it was only because he couldn't quite believe in her love for him. Because past experience had taught him to be wary, to expect treachery at every turn, the lack of faith had actually been in himself. He hadn't been able to believe that any woman could love him enough to be true. Caught up in the passion of her own anger and pain, she had been too blind to see what lay behind his quick suspicions.

What was it Maggie had asked? Did she love him enough to forgive him, enough to work out their differences? As far as she could see, the only thing that needed working on was Tony's faith in himself. If there were still more doubts and suspicions in the future, surely, guided by her love and fresh understanding, she could patiently knock them down one by one until Tony could finally be brought to the assurance that his trust in her was not misplaced.

Lisa realized abruptly that she was wasting time. She hurried back inside and, reaching for the phone again, with her heart pounding hard from excitement and a little bit of fear as well, she made three quick telephone calls. Afterward, she repacked her bag, closed up the house and within the hour was on her way south. Soon she was either going to end up with egg on her face and look like a pitiful fool or would become the happiest woman alive. Only time—and Tony's reaction—would tell.

At six o'clock Friday morning Tony groaned and rolled over to shut off the intrusive jangling of his alarm clock.

All week he'd slept badly and it was catching up with him.
Last night he had been awake until after three. His
tortured thoughts had kept sleep at bay as he'd worried
constantly about Lisa's disappearance. It wasn't good for
her to go off alone when no one knew where she was; he
knew that if any harm came to her, he would never forgive
himself as long as he lived. His rash condemnation had
driven her away and the guilt and anxiety he felt was an
unceasing nightmare.

Over and over she'd proved to him by her actions that
she loved him and yet right up to the bitter end he'd gone
on suspecting her every move, never quite believing her,
never trusting her honesty. Yet she'd always played fair
with him. Except for her threat to write about him without
his approval that first day at the ranch, she'd never told
him anything but the truth, and even after that, she had
made a point to come to him and tell him it had been an
empty threat. Pain slashed through him, remembering.
That had been the night they had first made love, right
here in this house, in this bed.

Because he couldn't bear such thoughts now, Tony
threw back the covers, got swiftly to his feet and went into
the bathroom for his shower. But even the sharp sting of
the water spraying across his body failed to make him feel
any better and when, afterward, he stood before the
mirror to shave, he had to grimace with distaste at the
sight that met his eyes. It wasn't his haggard appearance
that bothered him, though that was bad enough. His eyes
were red-rimmed from lack of sleep and the rest of his
face looked sort of gray. It was the sight of himself that

displeased him, for he was looking at the face of a
hot-tempered fool who had lost the best thing that had ever
come his way. If he had hurt Lisa so badly that she had felt
compelled to run away so that even her closest friends
didn't know where she was, there seemed about as much
chance for him to ever win her back as there was for him
to turn back time itself. It was utterly impossible.

Back in the bedroom, Tony chose a dark suit for the day
and began to dress. When it came to the pale-silver tie, he
went to stand before the dresser mirror, but this time he
avoided his eyes as he concentrated on knotting the strip
of silk. Then, snatching up the jacket to his suit, he headed
down the hall and into the kitchen.

Although he wasn't hungry, he forced himself to eat
breakfast. He had a business luncheon to attend today, but
it would be a late one.

He had just finished eating when the phone rang. Tony
leapt eagerly to answer it. Surely no one would be calling
this early . . . except perhaps Lisa!

But the hope died as he answered the phone: the caller
was Maggie.

"I'm at the airport hangar, Tony," she said immediately. "There's a problem and you'd better come at once!"

Utterly confused, Tony could scarcely even think for an
instant. "What is it?" he asked. And then, more sharply,
"What're you doing in Los Angeles? What're you doing
at the hangar?"

"I can't discuss it now," Maggie said. "Just come,
Tony. Come!"

The phone went dead in his hand. Tony dropped it and

stared blankly through the window at the ocean for a moment, totally baffled. *What in the hell was going on?* Maggie hadn't made a bit of sense.

But there had been an underlying urgency in her voice and that alone galvanized him into action. She needed him and that was all he had to know. Standing around trying to guess what was going on was a waste of time. Tony snatched up his jacket and rushed out of the house to his car.

The traffic congestion today was hideous and Tony's anxiety and impatience made him feel as though he were moving at a snail's pace. Meanwhile, speculation ran riot and he imagined all sorts of horrible things. Something wrong with Maggie herself; something wrong with Bill. That must be it, he thought tensely. Something awful had happened to Bill, and Maggie had come here to use his private plane to get to him in New York faster than a commercial plane could carry her. She probably wanted Tony to accompany her as well.

Or Lisa, he thought suddenly. Had something happened to Lisa? When he'd told Maggie what Roni had said, that Lisa wanted nothing more to do with him, she'd said she was going to try to reach her, even though he'd forbidden her to interfere. Not that that would stop Maggie, if she felt what she was doing was right, Tony realized. So was that it? Did she know where Lisa was? His heart thundered with fear and his frustration with the traffic grew to an intolerable level.

When he reached the airport hangar at last, he saw his plane at once out on the tarmac, obviously ready for akeoff. Maggie must have ordered it to be prepared. Tony's mouth was as dry as cotton as he raced toward it.

Just as he reached the steps, his pilot came to the door. "What is it?" he gasped. Every nerve in his body was taut with a horrible dread.

"The lady's inside, sir. I'd better let her tell you herself. If you're ready, we'll be taking off just as soon as we get clearance from the tower."

Tony was at the top of the steps by now. He nodded numbly and, expecting the worst, passed by the other man and opened the door to the private cabin.

There was only one occupant in the cabin and Maggie was nowhere to be seen. What met his stunned gaze instead was an exquisite vision of loveliness. Lisa sat calmly in one of the wide, comfortable chairs, hands clasped in her lap, and she was wearing the most beautiful white dress Tony had ever seen. It had long, sheer full sleeves, a wide skirt and a high-necked top with dainty seed pearls on it. Her gorgeous hair, glinting like copper streaked with gold, was swept back behind one ear by some sort of flower made out of pearls as well. The sight of her at all was astonishing enough when he'd been expecting Maggie and a terrible emergency, but to see her looking so graceful and enchanting almost bowled him over.

He didn't speak at once. He couldn't. His throat felt too tight and he was still too stunned. He continued to stare, scarcely believing the evidence before his eyes after the nightmarish week of longing and fear. He had begun to believe he would never see her again and now to find her looking so absolutely lovely, regal as a princess . . . it took his breath away.

Lisa's lips curved into the softest of smiles. As she did, he dimly became aware of the revving up of the plane's engines. In a few more minutes they would be airborne.

The shock was wearing off and Tony suddenly realized he didn't know either why he was here or where he was going.

"Do you mind clueing me in on why you commandeered my plane?"

Lisa stood up. "I'd be happy to. I'm kidnapping you."

Tony quirked an eyebrow at her. "Kidnapping?"

She nodded. "That's right."

The tension that had been in him ever since Maggie's call suddenly drained away as Tony realized some sort of joke had been played on him. The relief was overwhelming, but with it came a surge of anger. He trembled in reaction. "I've been half out of my mind with terror ever since Maggie's call," he said in a voice that still shook with trauma. "I imagined you or Bill dead . . . or at the least, injured. The pair of you had better have a damn good explanation for the agony I've just been through!" His gaze swept around the cabin and he growled, "Where the hell *is* Maggie, anyway?"

"By now I suppose she's at your beach house in Malibu," Lisa said, surprising him further. "You probably passed each other on the way. I'm truly sorry you were frightened, Tony. I guess we didn't think how that call would affect you. But you're not to be angry with Maggie. I'm responsible for everything and she only made that call to you because I asked her to do it."

"Did you ask her to order my plane ready for flight, too?" he demanded.

Lisa nodded, but did not elaborate.

Tony's eyes narrowed as he frowned and exasperation tinged his voice. "So far you're not doing a very good job of explaining a damn thing," he said harshly, "and my patience is fast running out. Why are we on this plane and why is Maggie at my house?"

Lisa quaked inwardly, hoping he couldn't see how nervous she really was. Now came the hard part . . . the moment of truth. What had seemed like a good idea at the time now seemed outlandishly absurd and it was going to be harder than she had thought. Somehow, in all her planning, she'd never once dreamed they would frighten Tony so badly. Now he was furious about that and she honestly couldn't blame him. Because he had been so shaken, he was far from receptive and that didn't augur well for the success of her plan.

The plane suddenly began to taxi and it threw them both off-balance so that they collided. Tony's arms shot out to save her from falling and their eyes met. It seemed to Lisa that time itself stopped as they gazed silently at each other. The unresolved questions and anxieties in both their eyes were apparent, as were the hurts and the hopes.

"I think," Tony said with a husky catch to his voice, "we'd better sit down." He drew her with him to the sofa, but once they were seated he removed his hands from her arms and Lisa felt bereft.

Still, he didn't seem quite as angry as before. He leaned back against the cushions and stretched out one arm across the back, so that his body was angled toward hers. Their knees brushed together as he asked in a calm voice, "Now, do you mind telling me what's going on and why I've been kidnapped? As your hostage, I assume you're expecting some sort of payoff. What are your demands for my freedom?"

If she hadn't spotted the telltale gleam of humor in his eyes just then, Lisa wasn't sure she would have had the courage to go through with it after all. But she did see it and it bolstered her nerve.

"Your freedom," she said boldly, watching him carefully for his reaction, "is nonnegotiable."

"Is that right?" He looked interested but not unduly alarmed. "May I inquire what is, then?"

"Nothing. I'm making you my prisoner for life." Lisa's heart pounded as she dared to put it into words.

He was catching on, she could tell. His mouth twitched while he pretended to think. "What," he asked with mock seriousness, "are my chances for parole or at least time off for good behavior?"

"Absolutely nil," she assured him solemnly.

Tony sighed dramatically. "What a hard-hearted captor you are. In that case, I suppose I'll just have to adjust and make the best of a bad situation, won't I?"

In one swift motion, his arms were around her, pinning her back against the cushions, and she was being ruthlessly kissed. His lips moved over hers, fiercely demanding, as though during the days they had spent apart he had become starved for the taste of her. A spreading warmth enveloped Lisa as her own arms went around his waist, drawing him closer.

Her lips parted beneath the fiery possession of his and

his hunger seemed to increase at the soft yielding. One hand pressed against the nape of her neck, as though he were the captor and she his prisoner. And indeed she was—a prisoner of the love she felt for him. It had driven her to the desperate, insane measures she had taken this day.

Tony's need of her as well was also apparent by the intensity of his kiss and the urgent pressure of his hands. It was a kiss like no other they had ever shared. It spoke of everything that needed to be said and clarified between them—of apologies and regrets, of gladness and hope, of loving and promises . . . and most of all, of trust. It was a moment of highly charged emotional commitment that while enhancing physical passion went far beyond it, deeper and deeper until it reached the essence of their beings.

It left them both trembling and breathless and for an eternity afterward they simply gazed at each other in mute eloquence.

"I love you." Tony's voice came at last, ragged and soft. His thumb rubbed in a tender, semicircular motion against the back of her neck. "I've been crazy this past week," he whispered, "thinking I'd lost you for good."

"I love you, too," Lisa said unsteadily. The love was evident in her eyes.

"Darling, I'm sorry I—"

Lisa lifted her hand and clasped it gently over his lips. "I know. I know," she said softly. "So am I. It's behind us now. Let's forget it."

"I can't." Tony kissed her hand and removed it. His voice was husky and thick with regret. "I realize now how much I hurt you and how wrong I was. I should have trusted you and known that you were telling me the truth that day. God knows I wanted to believe you, Lisa, but I guess I just never quite learned how to believe in anyone. But if you'll just bear with me, I'll learn. I swear I'll never hurt you again. You're the only thing that has any meaning in my life and if I lose you, I'll have nothing."

Lisa smiled tremulously. "I told you you're my prisoner for life, remember?" she asked, teasing him. "You're not going to lose me, Tony, not ever. Unless you break the trust I've placed in you today. If you do, I'm going to be horribly embarrassed."

A smile softened his face. "Ah, back to the kidnapping," he said with satisfaction. "Just what have you got in store for me?"

"Well, first you're being abducted to Las Vegas, where I expect you to behave obediently like a docile prisoner should and marry me at once."

A fire began to dance in Tony's eyes. "Sweet torture," he said with relish. "Tell me more."

"Next we fly straight back to Los Angeles and drive to Malibu where we'll have our wedding reception at your house. My parents arrived last night and this morning my mother is helping Roni and Maggie get everything ready while Jack and my father go to the airport to meet Maggie's son Bill."

"Hmmm. Confiscated my personal property as well," Tony muttered beneath his breath. "You are some band of outlaws indeed! What about my office and the business appointments I had scheduled for today? Did anyone think about that?"

Lisa nodded. "Oh, yes. Maggie's taking care of that. She's to tell your secretary that you had an urgent personal matter to attend to and instruct her to cancel all your appointments for the next two weeks. Of course she will be told that you'll be calling in on Monday to check on things."

"Kind of you both," Tony said dryly. "I'm glad to hear my business won't collapse entirely. Just as a matter of curiosity, where will I be for the next two weeks?"

"At my uncle's house on Lake Tahoe where it's quiet and secluded. That's where I went this week. I think you'll like it."

"Hmmm, where else would a mermaid want to go except near a body of water?" Tony murmured. "I should have guessed. But if it's secluded, it sounds like it has definite possibilities." His lips came enticingly close to hers. "And what fate do you have planned for me there? A sentence of hard labor?"

"Precisely." Lisa's arms curled around his neck and she felt a little giddy and intoxicated by his nearness. "Think you can hold up under the strain of having to make love to me every day?" she asked, giving him the most seductive smile she could produce.

Tony's grin matched the laughter in his eyes. He pulled her closer and promised huskily, "I'll do my best."

"That's all I can ask," she whispered just before her lips met his in a kiss that while less emotionally intense than the preceding one, was certainly no less passionate.

When they drew apart a long time later, Lisa's anxiety suddenly reasserted itself in spite of Tony's loving smile. "Do you really want to do this, Tony?" she couldn't help asking with a tiny wistful note to her voice. "I know all my arrangements have been a bit heavy-handed, but if you still have any doubts about marrying me, please tell me now while there's time to call it off. I really don't want to go through with it unless you're completely certain in your own mind that you want it, too."

Only then did Tony fully understand why she had chosen to present him with such an outrageously unique plot. She had placed herself squarely in a vulnerable position, putting not pressure but full trust in him. It was her way of showing him that if she had this much faith in him, while leaving him the option of rejecting her and thus humiliating her in the eyes of all the people they both cared about most, he could, in turn, give her all his trust with perfect confidence. She had put her love on the line, laying herself wide open for the very real possibility of his refusal in order to prove to him once and for all just how much she did love him. With that realization, the ghosts of the past were put behind him for good, and Tony was a bit shaken at the knowledge that he was the recipient of such generous love.

He cleared his throat and tried to conceal the depths of his emotions. "Hey! Hey, lady captor, don't blow it now!" he chided gently. "Don't you know you're never supposed to show any doubts or indecisiveness in front of a prisoner? Besides," he added with a distinct twinkle in his eyes, "I'm rather looking forward to that hard-labor camp. I intend to apply myself diligently to the task. But for all your superorganizational skills, there seems to be one little detail that you overlooked during your planning."

"What's that?" Lisa asked dreamily, quite content now that she knew for certain she hadn't made a ghastly mistake after all.

"The rings. We're about to be married and we don't have any rings."

Lisa's eyes widened and her mouth puckered into a circle. "Oh, no!" she exclaimed softly in dismay. "And I thought I'd remembered everything!"

Tony chuckled. "No matter. We'll stop at a jeweler's on the way. How do matching bands sound to you?"

"Perfect," she told him.

"Later on we can shop for that engagement ring I'd planned on getting for you," Tony said against her lips.

"Oh, but I don't need—"

His lips silenced her before he murmured, "Don't argue with me. Even prisoners have some rights and I intend to exercise mine."

He moved away just enough so that he could gaze into her eyes and suddenly he began to laugh. It was deep and hearty, filled with genuine enjoyment.

Lisa's lips spread into a smile in response, even though she didn't know what he found so funny. "What's so amusing?" she asked.

"Just think what a story we'll have to tell our children someday. Mommy kidnapped Daddy, hijacked his own plane and forced him to marry her! With that kind of fiery spirit coursing through their blood, there's no telling what sort of outlandish tricks they'll pull!"

"True." Lisa laughed. "But won't it be fun to find out?"

Tony's laughter died away and the soft light in his eyes

made Lisa catch her breath. There was so much love within them that it swelled her heart almost to bursting.

"I can't imagine any greater pleasure," he said thickly, "than to share the adventure of life with you and our children. Bad times or good, we'll be together always, Lisa, because I'll never let you go."

"Always," she vowed softly. What a lovely, permanent sound the word had! Her own eyes were shining with love. She tilted her head to receive his kiss as he bent toward her.

Just then there was the altered sound of the engines and a moment later they could feel the downward motion of the plane as it began the first stage of its descent toward the city in the desert.

They smiled at one another in the joyful certainty that before this morning was over, they would be man and wife. The rest of their lives would be rich with purpose and fulfillment because they would be together.